Haiku Holiday

How to Have Haiku Parties and Write Great Haikus

Jason Flick

Order this book online at www.trafford.com
or email orders@trafford.com

Most Trafford titles are also available at major online book retailers.

© Copyright 2014 Jason Flick.
All drawings are Jason Flick originals.
All rights reserved. No part of this publication may be reproduced, stored in a retrieval system, or transmitted, in any form or by any means, electronic, mechanical, photocopying, recording, or otherwise, without the written prior permission of the author.

Printed in the United States of America.

ISBN: 978-1-4907-3823-9 (sc)
ISBN: 978-1-4907-3824-6 (e)

Because of the dynamic nature of the Internet, any web addresses or links contained in this book may have changed since publication and may no longer be valid. The views expressed in this work are solely those of the author and do not necessarily reflect the views of the publisher, and the publisher hereby disclaims any responsibility for them.

Trafford rev.   06/25/2014

 www.trafford.com
North America & international
toll-free: 1 888 232 4444 (USA & Canada)
fax: 812 355 4082

DEDICATED TO MY DAD

ACKNOWLEDGEMENTS

I owe a debt of gratitude to many friends, foes, lovers, leavers, landlords, landladies, leaping ladies, educational institutions, governmental institutions, institutional institutions, airlines, hotels, hostels, hostiles, beatniks, campers, deadheads, deadbeats, and bead makers... parking lot attendants, bountiful bosses, but not bad bosses, pawn shops, porn shops, and pet shops... and donut shops. There are a lot of people to thank for providing knowledge, experience, entertainment, inspiration, and a place to crash... sometimes literally.

In random order, muchas gracias to: God, Jesus Christ, Mom, Dad, Relatives, USA, Illinois, Grandma Alice, Henry T, Joe H, Big Jim O, Giovanna C, Robert DeNiro, Mia B, Lou F, Earl T, Greg C, Heidi M, Evan V, Jane C, Aaron D, Trafford Publishing, Book Expo America, Jenkins Group, Isabela, Espanha, Continental Airlines, Chuck, California, Jamie W, Barry R, Kristen C, Kristen P, Kristen S, Kirsten S, Laurie K, Marcelo L, The Firefly, Chicago, Ross L, Betty Page, Charles Bukowski, Last Exit, Erik D, Kai J, Robin R, Karen T, Kirsten H, Campaigners for Christ, Humberto L, B3 and Becky D in NYC, CBGB, The Talking Heads, The Ramones, Richard C, Steve S, Dalvinder S, John Malkovich, Eastern Illinois University, Janet L, Sue S, Senor Aguado y Senor Martin, The Sex Pistols, Public Image Limited, University of Missouri, Kansas City, The Record Bar, IRS Records, Thomas Hart Benton, Grant Wood, Jackson Pollock, Orlando, Florida, John B, Amy B, Ashford University, Kathleeeen K, Uncle Bob, Robert Zimmerman, Marcelo, Fabrizio L, Christine B, Kory, Joyce F, Gary and Kiki P, Mel Gibson, Mel Brooks, Rachel J, Andrew P, The Falcon Institute, The Goethe Institute, Route 66, New York City, Bleaker Street, Tripmaster Monkey, WEIU-FM, Washington Square Park, Rio de Janeiro, Lisbon, Portugal, The Pavilion, Terry L, Rob K, Becky A, Steve H, Strayer University, Gary B, Young Life, Holly A, Holly D, Niki F, Julia S, John Deere,

Augustana College, John Hughes, Seinfeld, Matthew Broderick, Claudia A, Kate F, Kate, Luciana G, Megan L, Becky and Jeff, Gina R, Nancy D, Nancy P, and Nancy E, Cynthia M, Joe D, Jesus C, Elizabeth S, Chris G, Grant B, Brian K, Brad B, Jenny P, WWJD, Rusty E, Lori W, Jeff C, Brazil Jeff, Derek E, Jason S, Steven Spielberg, George Lucas, The Pixies, Sarah Jessica Parker, Oprah Winfrey, Kristen Davis, Rotary International, Lutheran Youth Organization, Nancy K, Barb G, USA, Guanajuato, Mexico, Sterling, Illinois, Moline High School, Jerry Seinfeld, Lenny Bruce, Conan O'Brien, David Letterman, Matt M, Jimmy Fallon, Jimmy Kimmel, Sarah Silverman, Eddie Peppitone, Tom Cruise, Woody Allen, Valeria A, Brandy R, Jason H, Camp A, Sue W, President Barak Obama, Martin Luther, Socrates, U2, Island Records, Bob Marley, Ziggy Marley, Jana R, Crazy Canadians, Alexandra F, Randy G, Randy M, Jack D, Jack Kerouac, Adam Sandler, Dennis Farina, Niki F, J.D. Salinger, Walden University, Pity and Paty, Central Casting, William Burroughs, Alan Ginsburg, Karl F, Matthew Perry, The Parlor, Amanda D, Chesterfield's Paris, Einstein, Jim F, Kendra S, Chico, Mark W, Star 98.5, TEC, Jeff W, Tony S, Joe V, Marcus W, Svea, Danielle VD, The Wesley Foundation, John Wesley, Matt B, Fran Drescher, The Cosby Show, Liz K, Jeff V, Mark K, Jenn W, Maastricht, Netherlands, Van Gogh, Drew Barrymore, Leipzig, Germany, J.S. Bach, Elaine F, The Speakeasy, St. Ambrose University, The Republic, Jimmy Hendrix, The Clash, Tower Records, The Violent Femmes, Jennifer Grey, Bombay Sapphire Gin Lisa Fox, Angela G, Belgium Danny, Danny Aiello, Gunther, Steve Jobs, Jars of Clay, Donald Trump, The Learning Annex, The Waterboys, Funeral Party, Bill M, Leslie C, RIBCO, INXS, Pastor P, Sue I, Ralph S, Lars M, Quito, Ecuador, Colegio Americano, The Magic Bean, Drew D, Mark Burnett, The Strand, Chris G, Hoboken, New Jersey, Frank Sinatra, Dean Martin, Liza L, Dan H, Troy R, Count Basie, Max Roach, Pablo Picasso, The Amigos, Roy, The Newman Center, Mary and Roy L, Bruce P, Margarita L, Christiano S, The Lighthouse, Stephanie P, Matt B, Cooper, Michael Lembeck, Matt W, Kyle R, Chris S, Chris R, Matt G, Megan K, Black Hawk College, Flip, Australian Katherine, Cal H, Mike and Jean S, Wes H, David K, Sex in The City, Joe D, Boyd, Derek S, Mike F, Chi R, David F, Doug F, Mark J, Don S, The Beatles, Carlos Da F, Burton D, Dennis Miller, The Green Mill, Time Magazine, The Black Keys, J.C. The Sons of Thunder, Rosa M, and lots of other people man. Thanks for the good advice, good times, good intentions, and goodies.

CONTENTS

Preface x
Pre-Disclaimer 1
   #1: JUDGEMENT: Disclaimer Haiku 1
Disclaimer (Please read; witty and informative) 2
Overture 6
   #2: OPINION: Haiku Book 7
   #3: RELATION: Haiku Inception 7

Introduction 8
   Picture: Ash Face 8
   #4: EDUCATION: Free Sample 10
      What is a Haiku? 10
      The Great Haikus 12
      The 102… I Mean, 64 Great Ideas 14
      The Great Haikus… Again 15
      Used Cars 16
   #5: CHANCE: Used Cars For Sale… Cheap! 18
   #6: CITIZEN: Flat Tire 18
      Internet Hookey 26
      Pursuit of Happiness 26
   #7: HAPPINESS: The Pursuit of Beer and Popcorn 28
   #8: LIFE AND DEATH: All The World's A Stage
      (Late Night T.V.) 29

Day One: Thursday
   Picture: Lit Lady 36
   #9: BEAUTY: Bouncing Betty Page 37
   #10: ART: Smart Art (3D Art) 38
   #11: LOVE: Haiku Heaven 42
   #12: MATTER: A Bad Example (Big Boobs) 44
   #13: WEALTH: Trash Or Treasure (Spuma) 45
   #14: LAW: Haiku Ten Commandments 46
   #15: STATE: The Grifty Fifty 49
   #16: MEMORY: Class of 99 (Repeal Drinking Age!) 51

#17: LIBERTY/FREEDOM: Prohibition Beer (Road Trip)....53
    Green Mill Prohibition Poetry Slam (Chicago)................56
#18: VIOLENCE: Green Mill Girl Poetry Slam (Beatniks)....57
#19: JUSTICE: Just Ice Beer (Bacon and Beer/ Police Stop)....60
    Emergency Meditation 65

Day Two: Friday
Picture: Happy Harry..68
I Failed, No You Failed!..69
#20: EMOTION: Sex Pistols and Anger Management............70
#21: EQUALITY: Rainbow Beer (Candy Beer).......................71
#22: HABIT: Freud's Frolic (Cigars) 73
#23: WISDOM: Shining Moon (Cookies and Beer)...............73

Day Three: Saturday
Picture: Funny Hat Man 75
#24: REASONING: Haiku Philosophe (Rene Descartes) 76
#25: BEING: The Stinker (Poop Haiku) 76
    Butt Cake 76
#26: LABOR: Food for Thought (Poop Haiku 2) 77
#27: SIN: Flushing Your Sins (Poop Haiku 3)....................... 77
    Beer Cake 77
    Dehydrated Liquid Bread Bread (Beer Bread).........78
    Captain's Courageous 82
#28: LANGUAGE: Lingua Franca (Where's the Bathroom?) ...83
#29: FAMILY: Viva Zapata (Don't Drink the Water)............85
#30: PLEASURE AND PAIN: Smoking Beer
    (A Beer and a Blunt) 87
#31: GOOD AND EVIL: Vacuuming Vonnegut's Vomit........89

Day Four: Sunday
Picture: Peppy Paul...94
Walt Whitman 95
#32: HONOR: Full of Ships..97
#33: REVOLUTION: Breakfast Beer (Boston Tea Party) 98
#34: DEMOCRACY: Democracy Beer (Chocolate Beer) 101
    Margaret Atwood 103
#35: PUNISHMENT: Jail Cell Blues 104
    Christianity Part I 104

God's Library 106
#36: RELIGION: Holy Haiku (Matthew 6:9) 108
#37: MAN: Summer Beer-Aid (Big Juicy Nipples) 108
#38: CAUSE: Do The To Do 110
    The To Do List 112
#39: TIME: The Hourglass (Time Travel) 113
#40: IMAGINATION: Donut Hole (Beer and Donuts) 115

Day Five: Monday

Picture: George On Break 118
Sup Salinger? 119
#41: TYRANNY: Salinger Soup (War Machine) 121
#42: WORLD: Fish N Chips Ale (U.S. Fish Sticks and Beer) 123
    Certainly Cervantes 126
#43: VIRTUE AND VICE: Cervantes Cerveza 128
    Emergency Salsa 130
    Hypnotic Quixotic 131
    Hypnotic Quixotic (Poem) 132
    Renewable Energy Revolution 133
#44: PROGRESS: Renewable Energy Revolution
(Free Cocaine!) 134
    Ingenius U. 136
#45: CONSTITUTION: Fuck Off… Please
(Backwards Flush) 137
    Progress and Evolution 139
#46: EVOLUTION: Smart Phone Phony
(Digital Swiss Army Knife) 142
    Password Pissed 144
#47: EXPERIENCE: Password Poop 145
    God and Science, Faith and Reason 146
    Proof of the Eternity 149
    God and Music 149

Day Six: Tuesday: April Fool's Day

Picture: Feather In My Cap 151
#48: GOVERNMENT: April Fool's Day 152
    The American Brain Washing Machine 155
#49: SLAVERY: T.V. Time 157

#50: SENSE: Beer and Buns (Cinnamon Beer) 161
    Jean Paul Sartre 163
#51: WAR AND PEACE: Sartre Says… 164
    The Lord Said (Poem) 164
#52: NATURE: Ice Tea Beer (Peppermint Beer) 165
    Mark Twain 167
#53: TRUTH: Sawyer's Serendipity 174
#54: CHANGE: Siren Swan 175
    Emergency Prayer 175

Day Seven: Wednesday
    Picture: Bed Head 176
#55: ANIMAL: Pet My Pet Snake 177
#56: KNOWLEDGE: Forbidden Feast 179
    Forbidden Feast Recipe
    (Beer Macaroni and Cheese Tomato Soup) 182
#57: DUTY: Cleanliness Is Godliness… Sometimes
    (Dirty Dishes) 184
#58: SPACE: The Salt of the Sea (Hemingway's Harem) 186
    Salsa of the Sea (Tuna Salsa Snack) 189
    Christianity Part II 190
#59: POETRY: Bukowski's Bubbles
    (Peanut Butter and Jelly Beer) 193
    Jesus Joins the Mafia 196
    Why Should I be a Christian? 197
    A Simple Prayer 200
    Humility 201

Surprise!
    Picture: Laughing Langostino 202
#60: DESIRE: Buy-Sexual Beer (Oysters, Clams, and Beer) ... 203
    Henry Miller 206
#61: MIND: I Said What? (Cunt Lover) 207
    Denouement 208
    Exit Stage Left (Poem) 210
    Thinking Thoughts 212
    The Prickly Road (Poem) 213
    The Rope (Poem) 214

    Good News 215
    I Believe in Me (Poem) 216
    #62: WILL: Thank You Jesus 216

Post Script 217
    Picture: Drunk Puppy 217
    #63: SOUL: The Bottle of Christ (The Best Beer) 218
    #64: GOD: Unfinished 218

PREFACE

PRE-DISCLAIMER

WARNING: THIS BOOK IS WRITTEN FOR ADULTS. IT IS AT TIMES FILTHY AND VULGAR. IT IS LIKELY TO OFFEND. BUT, IT IS WRITTEN WITH GOOD INTENTIONS.

IT MAY MAKE YOU THINK, LAUGH, LEARN, AND GIVE YOU INSPIRATION.

#1: JUDGEMENT: DISCLAIMER HAIKU

(1)
Here's a disclaimer.
It will protect me and you.
Please use common sense.

DISCLAIMER

Hi. I just wanted to provide a few words of guidance and direction before you read this book, and to warn you of the contents. This book is an adult book. This book is intended for adult audiences. If this book were a movie, I'm sure that it would be rated R. It has dirty words, dirty jokes, sexual innuendos, sexual connotations, sexual positions... and beer (two things that I believe go well together). Is this book distasteful or vulgar? That is for you to decide for yourself. I believe that as free American citizens, we all have our own individual levels of tolerance for defining what is appropriate and what is inappropriate humor. If you are uncomfortable with something then please be my guest to skip it, or stop reading.

One of my favorite books is J.D. Salinger's *"Catcher in the Rye."* Many refer to it as simply, "Catcher". I read and loved that book as a Freshman in High School, and I don't remember if it was for a class, or for myself. In that book, the protagonist (hero), Holden Caufield, is an adolescent trying to be an adult. I recall one scene in which he visits a tavern as an under aged drinker and passes the time with ladies of the night (I imagine that is the edited version, and perhaps why it took ten years to write). This book is about an adult trying to be an adolescent (and recapture some of his youth in an effort to find himself). Although this is a book about poetry, it is also a fictional work of prose that will lead you on a journey of questions about yourself, and life, and climax with an inspiring end.

This book is filled with social satire and the opinions of the author. As the author, I am not a medical doctor, or a psychologist, or a lawyer, or a preacher, and I do NOT recommend that you try anything in this book. I also recommend that you take caution to practice safe sex, and to drink alcohol with restraint to avoid public intoxication and drinking and driving. Alcoholism and drinking and driving are serious problems with serious consequences and I have sympathy and empathy for those that have suffered these consequences.

This book contains social satire and occasional sarcasm and irony. However, I am an open minded and tolerant Christian that makes efforts to avoid offensive racism and judgement of other religious views and cultures. God bless America for being the secular and impartial "melting pot" of the World that provides for the freedom of speech and to practice your chosen religion. However, as a protestant Christian, I can attest that I am not being sarcastic, and that I am sincere in all of the passages regarding Christianity.

As for any other commentaries, the decision is up to the reader regarding my sincerity and whether to agree or disagree. Please feel free to agree or disagree with any of the content as I am an advocate of free speech and the free exchange of ideas. Any similarity to any other work, or references to personal individuals is coincidental as this is a work of original fiction, and is not intended to be for or about any particular individual. Basically, I don't give a "flying leap" what you do or think as long as it does not directly affect me.

About myself and my qualifications, I am an American Citizen, born in the United States from American parents. I have relatives and friends that are American Veterans. I was raised in the middle class in Middle America, (a.k.a. the Mid-West, or "Middle Earth" as contemporary people from the coasts sometimes call it). I do not currently have any official political affiliations or memberships. I am not now, nor have I ever been a member of the "Communist" party, or participated in any extremist or political activities. Some of my beliefs and convictions fall with the Left Wing, and some of my beliefs and convictions fall with the Right Wing. In general, I consider myself a political moderate and often appreciate the post 1960's "status quotient" America.

Regarding my qualifications and experience, I have been blessed with many great opportunities to experience foreign travel and culture (which in the past has been my "thing.") I have studied Spanish, Portuguese, and German, and I have traveled to Spain, Mexico, Ecuador, Brazil, Israel, Italy, China, France, the Netherlands, Germany, and other exotic destinations.
I believe these travels have provided an appreciation for the human experience and other cultures.

Jason Flick

For my undergraduate studies, I attended Eastern Illinois University, and completed a degree in Education. I studied and wrote papers with both conservative and left wing perspectives. For my graduate studies, I attended several American Universities and completed a Master of Arts at Ashford University.

Regarding my protestant Christian perspectives, I was baptized and confirmed in a Lutheran Church. In high school, I participated in ecumenical non-affiliated Christian Youth Groups, including the Roman Catholic, TEC (Teens Encounter Christ). As a Rotary International Exchange Student in high school, I attended a private Catholic School and attended and participated at a Catholic Church in Brazil. In college, I attended and participated in the Methodist church and youth group. I also attended and participated in and helped in fundraisers for the Roman Catholic Newman Center Youth Group. Although I consider myself a protestant Christian, I an not anti-Catholic. In later years, I have also attended and participated as part of an Episcopalian Church, and a Charismatic, and a Pentecostal Holy Spirit Church.

This is silly, but just to let you know that I am not crazy, I am NOT Jesus Christ. Also, I am not a holy prophet. Nor am I the second coming of Jesus Christ, or the Jewish Messiah. I am also NOT the Anti-Christ. Although I believe in Miracles and the miraculous and mystical power of prayer, I do NOT consider myself to have special powers or to work miracles. I am not a pastor, or a priest, or a preacher, or a minister. I would consider myself a layman, or an advocate for The Christian Church in general.

Lastly, this book consists of my opinions. I have chosen to include a variety of beer brands to add to the authenticity of the work. This book was written with no corporate sponsorship or affiliations, and any commercial references are not intended to be indicative to the quality or purpose of the product or company. Any corporate or commercial references are made without harmful intent.

Oops, there's more. Chicks… be chilling! Regarding the ladies and feminism… and "homosessuality", although I may have allowed myself to make reckless and silly and potentially inappropriate and disrespectful comments in writing this, I do not mean to be overtly offensive. Although I am currently a single heterosexual male, I appreciate human diversity and the right for women, and male and female homosexuals and bisexuals, and transgender individuals, to pursue their own interests and a happy life. I generally support women's rights and I am not opposed to gay marriage. I have dated women with a bisexual preference. I may have worked with or for homosexual men, or women.

There was a very popular cable television show around the year 2000 called "Sex in the City," about some liberated and independent working women that objectified men. That show portrayed only gay men as good men, and the rest were used as sex objects, or as stepping stones for power. Still, as a man, I often enjoyed that show. I hope that if you disagree or do not appreciate any of my humor, that you will let it slide for the purpose of entertainment.

In Summary, please don't drink and drive. Please be careful when you drink or smoke. Please do not attempt any of the activities contained in this book, or any illegal or potentially harmful activities in general. Please vote with your own political conscience. This book is a work of fiction and took more than a week to write and create. Please enjoy this book and practice common sense. Although I have enjoyed writing this book in a laissez faire pursuit of id, in real life I make efforts to be sophisticated and charming. May you have a long and blessed life, and may your farts smell like chocolate and roses (I don't know why you would eat roses)… God Bless You, and Cheers.

OVERTURE

Sunday, March 30, 2014

Greetings Mr. Thomas,

"Make it new."
-Ezra Pound (American Poet)
(Quote found in Jones and Wilson, An Incomplete Education)

What is up Mr. Awesome?

I am replying as per your request regarding the discussed book proposal. I have indeed been busy. I just gave myself a "selfie" haircut last night, as I cut my own hair!
My Uncle Jack once told me, "The difference between a good haircut and a bad haircut… is about three days."

I am currently taking Master's courses from an online college, and the most touted benefit of online education is that you can take the classes at home in your underwear. Thus, this is what I am doing.

Ergo, this could be a potential book theme… "At Home in Your Underwear: What happens if you spend a week at home in your underwear?"

This, however, is not exactly the theme of my current book project, but I might indeed pose that question. Still, I am very excited about this new book project. I am so excited that I just invented a "typo word" (a tyrd?). "Excitied" is when one is too excited to type.

This new book that I propose is a book of humorous poetry to consist mostly of haikus. It should be called, "Haiku Holiday: How to have haiku parties; and write great haikus."

It will be a book about spending a week of free time writing haikus about what happens during that week. For example, the title itself… IS A HAIKU!!!

I have already started writing it, and I think it has great potential. In fact… this letter is going to be in the book.

#2: OPINION: HAIKU BOOK

(1)
I'm writing a book
It's about writing haikus.
You're going to love it!

Well, Mr. T, that's what the book is. So, let's keep in contact and I will let you know how it is going and what is happening on my… "Haiku Holiday"

#3: RELATION: HAIKU INCEPTION

(1)
I send Best Regards.
I hope it will be a hit!
Or, at least a book.

Cheers,
Jason Flick

INTRODUCTION

ASH FACE

INTRODUCTION

WHAT HAPPENS WHEN A STRUGGLING AUTHOR AND STUDENT IS BEING FOLLOWED BY THE COPS AT THE END OF HIS PROBATION? HE TAKES A "HAIKU HOLIDAY" AND SPENDS A WEEK AT HOME IN HIS UNDERWEAR DRINKING BEER, SMOKING CIGARS, AND WRITING HAIKUS. WILL HE MANAGE TO PASS HIS CLASS? WILL HE FIND LOVE ON THE INTERNET? WILL HE SELL HIS CAR SO HE CAN PAY HIS BILLS? WILL HE FIND TRUTH AND THE MEANING OF LIFE? WILL HE SUCCEED IN GAINING HIS FREEDOM? FIND OUT WHAT HAPPENS WHEN ONE MAN TAKES A JOURNEY OF SELF DISCOVERY ON A... HAIKU HOLIDAY?

It is my belief that the most wonderful aspect about research is the unlimited potential for topics and discovery. In my opinion, the concept of research itself revolves around three things... curiosity, questions, and the need to know. Any and all significant research should include all three of these elements: curiosity, questions, and the need to know. The question that I aspire to research is, What happens if a person dedicates a week of free time to writing free association and spontaneous haiku poetry? The answer is... a "Haiku Holiday!"

> "[I resolve to] no longer to seek any other science than the knowledge of myself, or of the great book of the world."
> -Rene Descartes
> (Quote taken from Fadiman, The Lifetime Reading Plan).

Although I am not going to spend a week in my underwear (as much as I would enjoy that), I will indeed be spending a week largely "hiding out" at home and trying to focus on writing haikus. I will write haikus while hanging out with myself, and getting to know myself, (probably getting intimate with myself... at least a little bit).

Although this is a book about poetry, it is also a fictional work of prose that will lead you on a journey of questions about yourself, and life, and climax with an inspiring end. Can man achieve enlightenment and overcome selfish impulses through education and experience? Probably yes. I should think so. But, can man achieve enlightenment and overcome selfish impulses and achieve the Socratic mandate of Socrates, to "Know Thyself!" by spending a week of writing haiku poems? This is... what I will discover during the next week while I take a... Haiku Holiday.

#4: EDUCATION: FREE SAMPLE

(1)
This is a haiku.
You might learn a thing, or two,
If you read this poo.

WHAT IS A HAIKU?

What is a haiku? A haiku is described by The American Heritage Dictionary of The English Language in the following adapted definition:

Haiku: (hi-koo) noun, plural, haiku, also haikus. 1. A Japanese lyric verse form having three unrhymed lines of five, seven, and five syllables, traditionally invoking an aspect of nature or the seasons. 2. A poem written in this form. [Japanese : hai, amusement (from Chinese pa, farce) + ku, sentence (from Chinese ju).]
- American Heritage Dictionary, Third Edition, 1992

Well, as the author, I find this interesting, because I learned a few things myself about haikus, and I wrote this book! I must confess, sadly, I'm writing this segment after I already wrote most of the book... and, it turns out, there's some stuff that I didn't even know about haikus. I knew that a haiku is a Japanese poem of three lines of 5, 7, and 5 syllables.

Haiku Holiday

I did NOT know that haiku means amusing poem in Japanese. I also did not know that the haiku is not supposed to rhyme. Some of my haikus might rhyme. However, I will invoke a caveat loophole, in that since my haikus are written in English... they would not rhyme in Japanese. I also did not know that there is a Chinese version, Pa-Ju. It seems that just like everything else these days, the haiku was made in China.

What the hell is a syllable? A syllable is described in the following definition adapted from The American Heritage Dictionary of The English Language:

Syllable: (sil-e-bel) noun, 1. Linguistics. A. A unit of spoken language consisting of a single uninterrupted sound formed by a vowel, dipthong, or syllabic consonant alone, or by any of these sounds preceded, followed, or surrounded by one or more consonants. 2. The slightest bit of spoken or written expression.
        - American Heritage Dictionary, Third Edition, 1992

What is a dipthong? I know that a thong bikini is a tiny bikini bottom used as swimsuits and underwear that has a tiny strap in the back that barely lines the crack of the buttocks. For men, these are called "banana hammocks", and for ladies they are called "G-strings." People wear then to show off a hot bod, and to get a better tan line. In Brazil, happily, these are very popular, and they are called "fio dental," or "dental floss."

I think a dipthong is when you have two vowels together. Basically a syllable is the shortest spoken part of a word. There are individual letters, then syllables, then words, then sentences, then paragraphs, etc. Basically, a syllable is a vowel between two consonants. For example, the word, "slut" has one syllable. The word "slutty" has two syllables. The word, "fornicate" has three syllables (for-ni-cate) because the last letter e is silent. The word fornication has four syllables (for-ni-ca-shen). It is basically, the smallest division of spoken parts of a word.

Now, I have another caveat loophole to invoke. For the purpose of this book, I have also taken the liberty to use the modern colloquial "American" pronunciation of English words to determine the syllables for the haikus. For example, the word "different", technically has three syllables (diff-er-ent). But, when spoken, most people in America take a short cut, and use a 2 syllable pronunciation (Diff-rent). Perhaps this is because Americans are very efficient and innovative, or if you're British, you could claim we're lazy.

Also, for the purpose of writing this book… I was often drinking substantially, and I may have been occasionally "intoxicated," and taken a few liberties in my haikus as a result. There may be a few mistakes of four, or six, or eight syllables. If this bothers you, taken a lesson, and "don't drink and write!"

Also, for stylistic purposes, I have not bothered to put my name after every haiku. However, unless referenced otherwise, all of the poems in this book have been composed by myself.

Lastly, it is interesting to note, that an unintentional paradox, is that this book has used the Eastern and Asian format of the Chinese, and Japanese haiku, to communicate my reflections on the Mortimer Adler selection of Western concepts from The Great Books Movement. As such, this book serves as an example of how different cultures can collaborate, communicate, innovate, and co-exist in harmony and produce… mediocre results.

Haiku Holiday: An excuse, or raison d'etre, for spending a weekend, or week, at home in your underwear, writing poetry, smoking cigars, doing dishes, getting fucked up on beer, and hiding from the cops.
- Jason Flick, Compendium Of Chosen Knowledge, 2013

THE GREAT HAIKUS

Mortimer J. Adler is widely known as the pioneer and leader of "The Great Books Movement." In the 19th century, liberal arts higher education consisted largely of studying "The Classics" of Western Literature, Philosophy, and Science. At the end of the 19th century, Penguin Publishing created their "Classics" Series, and Harvard President, Charles Elliot, compiled a group of classic works called the "Five Foot Shelf". Later, in the 1920's, Mortimer Adler received the torch of Western Civilization when studying at Columbia University,

Haiku Holiday

while in John Erskine's "General Honors" course. Then Adler and Robert Hutchins began the Great Books Movement at the University of Chicago.

"The Idea of including all students is, in fact, what Adler and Hutchins originally had in mind, although they began with a small and select group. Not only did they want to make great books a requirement for all University of Chicago undergraduates, but throughout their careers they spoke in favor of democratizing education and providing strong liberal education, including reading great books, for the masses. (Casement, 2002, p.11)"

At the University of Chicago, Adler brought together Robert Hutchins, John Erskine, Scott Buchanan, and Stringfellow Barr, to create the Encyclopaedia Britannica Company's *"Great Books of the Western World"* Series. In the 1950's Adler was part of Chicago's "Great Books Foundation," and then later helped lead the "Institute for Philosophical Research" funded by a grant from the Ford Foundation, and later with support and direction from Paul Hoffman, Robert Hutchins, Paul Mellon, and Arthur A Houghton, Jr. Later Adler continued The Great Books Movement through participation in The Aspen Institute for Humanistic Studies, also featuring the contributions of William Casement.

The Great Ideas Movement has grown and expanded to include many variations of mass media reading lists of great books, such as Clifton Fadiman's, *"The Lifetime Reading Plan."* Hundreds of academic institutions across America have taken inspiration from Adler's Great Ideas Movement to create programs focused on the Liberal Arts, The Humanities, and The Classics of Western Civilization. Some of these institutions include Notre Dame, Boston College, The University of Virginia, and Joseph Tussman's Berkeley experiment in the 1960's, as well as hundreds of others. Wilber Wright College has offered a four course certificate in The Great Books.

The Great Books Movement led to Adler's Explanation of the Result of the Great Books, which was "The Great Conversation", and "The Great Ideas". Many of today's "Classics" programs have been adapted to fit an interdisciplinary model, and are considered Liberal Studies.

The most recent academic trend in pursuing studies of "The Classics" and interdisciplinary studies, involves online research and education programs, and the digitization of Western Humanities related studies. This trend can be seen in the growth of Project Gutenberg, The Perseus Project, Project Bartleby, and Google Books. More information can currently be found at www.nas.org/new.html (Casement, 2002).

Before his unfortunate passing in 2001, Mortimer J. Adler wrote several books about "The Great Books," and "The Great Conversation," and "The Great Ideas." One of those prominent books, written with Charles Van Doren, was the best seller, "How to Read a Book." Another book written by Adler in 1981, was *Six Great Ideas.*"

In the book jacket, Adler states "It cannot be too often repeated that philosophy is everybody's business." That is why I have conspired to create a series of "Great Haikus" while pursuing a journey of self discovery; because, "Philosophy is everybody's business", and that includes me... dammit!

THE 102... I MEAN, 64 GREAT IDEAS

What are the Great Ideas? Adler explains the concept of The Great Ideas in this excerpt from, *Six Great Ideas.*

"The words that constitute the vocabulary of philosophical or human thought... numbered no more than a thousand words... "*The Great Ideas, A Syntopicon*" lists 102 such words... forty years ago... I and my colleagues thought 102 was the number we needed in order to delineate the discussion of the great ideas that occurs in the great books of Western Civilization. But now, with a different purpose in view, I think I can cut that number down to sixty four... My purpose now is to list the words that are in everyone's vocabulary, but that also name great ideas that everyone who has completed a basic, humanistic schooling, should be reasonably conversant with."

So, in essence, the following list of 64 words and ideas, are the simple version of the list of 102 Great Ideas from Western History.

Or, perhaps these 64 words could be considered the Great Ideas... For Idiots? Well, let us remember Adler's inspirational words that "Philosophy is everybody's business," and enjoy this simple list of The Great Ideas of Western Civilization.
Here are the 64 "Easy" Great Ideas taken from Adler's *"Six Great Ideas"*.

"Animal, Art, Beauty, Being, Cause, Chance, Change, Citizen, Constitution, Democracy, Desire, Duty, Education, Emotion, Equality, Evolution, Experience, Family, God, Good and Evil, Government, Habit, Happiness, Honor, Imagination, Judgement, Justice, Knowledge, Labor, Language, Law, Liberty (or Freedom), Life and Death, Love, Man, Matter, Memory, Mind, Nature, Opinion, Pleasure and Pain, Poetry, Progress, Punishment, Reasoning, Relation, Religion, Revolution, Sense, Sin, Slavery, Soul, Space, State, Time, Truth, Tyranny, Violence, Virtue and Vice, War and Peace, Wealth, Will, Wisdom, World!"

THE GREAT HAIKUS... AGAIN

What are the Great Haikus? The Great Haikus are the Haikus that I write during this journey of self discovery, or during this Haiku Holiday. Why are they great? They might not be so great. But, they will be great to me. And the idea of following the lead of Socrates, to "Know Thyself" and take some time to seek self discovery, THAT IS, I think, a Great Idea.

Thus, in homage to Mortimer J. Adler of The Great Books Movement, I bring you the... 64 Great Haikus!:

USED CARS

So, I have a plan to sell my car. I need to pay some bills. Here's how to sell a used car.

Step One: Clean Your Car.

So, the first step is to clean it up really good. So, I got everything out of it except the absolute necessities. I looked under the seats and found a couple dollars in change. I found some old ketchup packs and straws. I found some cassette tapes, (which is weird, because I don't have a tape player). I found a bunch of receipts. There is nothing worse than receipts. I try to keep mine for a while in case I have to return something. Sometimes a receipt can help bring back memories like a photograph. I should start a scrap book of receipts. Maybe that will be my next book; "Radical Receipts".

I found a deck of cards, some butane lighters, a couple of books, and some maps. And, I found some emergency food in the glove box that I forgot about; gum and beef jerky... and a small can of "potted meat." I don't even know what "potted meat is." I guess it's like "dog food", but for people. It's human dog food... in a can! But in an emergency, I guess I'd eat it.
I found a knife, a screwdriver, some work gloves, and a flashlight. Also, there was some old junk mail... and some bills. I don't know why I keep junk mail, or coupons. I never use them.
It's amazing how much crap you find in all of the little compartments, and pouches, and under the seats. Ear drops, candles, fingernail clippers, cologne, business cards, and pens. Don't ask me how I got candles in my car? I guess sometimes, I am a pack rat.

Haiku Holiday

I always thought... it was actually pretty tidy. Anyway, first you have to clean out everything! Then go to the carwash and wash it. Then vacuum it. Then, here is the secret to selling your car. You wash it, and vacuum it... again! And, end with a spot free rinse. Then, it will look almost like new. Then, you clean the windows, and dust the whole dashboard. Then, the finishing touch that will make it look brand new, is to wipe all of the plastic and vinyl surfaces with a car interior cleaner, and then wipe it with a car interior polish! Then, the car will look so good, you won't want to sell it.

Then, find a nice sunny place with a nice background, like a public park, and take some pictures (with the sun behind you.) Finally, tape a for sale sign in the back window, lock the doors, and park it in a safe place. Voila! You are ready to sell your car.

Step Two: Put An Ad In The Paper.

So, one of the best ways to sell a car, is to put an ad in the classified section of your local newspaper. You want to look up the value of your car on the internet, and shop to compare prices. Then, you have to make a list of all of the cool stuff your car has.

It has air conditioning, power steering, power windows, power locks, air bags, remote control digital television, refrigerator, wading pool, Vaseline dispenser, and camping toilet.
I'm joking about the power steering of course. However, you really can get all of that stuff for your car... at truck stops. Truck stops have the funniest crap for your car. You can get an oven for your car, a CB radio (citizen band), an air horn, a dashboard compass, and most importantly... fuzzy dice!

The funny thing is that car ads have a secret code to save space. Air conditioning, for example, is just, "air." And power locks, are "pwr locks." But, thankfully, the newspaper saleslady, or salesman will help you with that. Of course, you got to have a picture. Everyone wants a picture, and it gets more attention. You have to find out what year the car is, and how many miles it has on the speedometer. This will make a difference in how much the price of the car will be. Lastly, once you

Jason Flick

figure out how much your car is worth, you want to add a little extra. You always need to add a little extra, because people... ALWAYS, want a deal.

Also, I would try to get paid in cash, and be sure to tell them it is sold, "as-is". Maybe have them sign a piece of paper that says they bought the car "as-is", with the mileage, and how much they paid.

So, I cleaned the car, and I called an ad in. Now, all I have to do is sit and wait. Now, I sit and wait for the phone to start ringing. Come on phone... ring! Well, it usually takes a day, or two, for the ad to get listed in the paper. So, first, I will wait for the ad. Then, I will wait for the phone to ring.

In the meantime, here is a haiku that I wrote for the newspaper saleswoman. I sent here a text message from my phone, with this haiku, and pictures of the car. And, some pictures of my crotch (with my pants on).

#5: CHANCE: USED CARS FOR SALE... CHEAP!

(1)
Chris the saleswoman,
She will help me sell my car.
I'm going to be rich!

#6: CITIZEN: FLAT TIRE

(1)
How I got the money,
To pay for printing this book.
Here is what happened.

(2)
My car is for sale!
I'm asking a thousand bucks.
I hope it will sell.

Haiku Holiday

(3)
A thousand dollars,
Will help me pay for this book.
Then, I will be rich!

(4)
The first step to sell;
Place an ad in the paper…
Classified section.

(5)
I think it will sell…
Better with a picture ad.
I'll send it email.

(6)
I had a good lead.
We met at the grocery store.
They said, too much rust.

(7)
Then, on the way home,
A cop pulled up behind me.
My tags are expired.

(8)
I turned off the road,
At a Gyros restaurant,
And, I ate gyros.

(9)
Gyros is lamb meat.
It's a delicious sandwich.
It's pronounced Yee-Rose.

(10)
I did not get fries.
I already ate pizza,
At the gas station.

(11)
Then, I left for home.
But, I stopped by my post box.
There was just a bill.

(12)
Then, I hit the road;
Lonely, and dark… and no sale.
It started to rain.

(13)
But then, it got worse.
My driver's side tire blew out,
With ten miles to go.

(14)
I drove to the side.
I went to open the trunk.
I got the spare tire.

(15)
It was a doughnut.
That's a mini size spare tire…
Not a real doughnut.

(16)
It's temporary,
Until you get the tire fixed.
It doesn't last long.

(17)
So, just remember,
45 is the top speed,
For a hundred miles.

(18)
I got out the jack.
Then I took off the hub caps.
I jacked up the car.

(19)
Before the tire raised,
Left for loose, Right for tight.
I loosed the wheel nuts.

(20)
I jacked it higher.
Until, the wheel left the ground.
I took off the nuts.

(21)
It started to pour.
It was raining really hard.
And, my clothes were wet.

(22)
A man stopped to help.
I told him, "I'm almost done!"
"Good bye, and thank you."

(23)
He left, and I waived.
But then, the tire would not budge.
It would not come off.

(24)
I was embarrassed.
But, then a State Trooper stopped,
And, turned on his lights.

(25)
Now, I'm in trouble.
He's going to write a ticket,
For my expired plates.

(26)
I asked for a ride,
Back home to get a mallet,
To get the tire off.

(27)
I said, "it's for sale."
"And, I don't have the right tools."
"I normally do."

(28)
He gave me a ride.
We talked about speed limits.
It's now seventy.

(29)
I got the mallet…
Cereal, soda, cigars,
In case I was stuck.

(30)
He then took me back.
Luckily, the rain then stopped.
I asked to be dropped.

(31)
I then said, "Good bye,"
And, offered him a soda.
He said, "I'll stop back."

(32)
My blinkers were on.
They're the safety hazard lights,
That warn other cars.

(33)
The nuts in pocket,
I took the mallet with me.
The ground was still wet.

(34)
I laid on the ground.
Then, I crawled under the car.
I hit the wheel hard.

(35)
"Yeah!" It came loose.
I pulled the tire off the rim.
But, it bumped the jack.

(36)
The jack... slowly tipped,
And, I watched the car fall down!
"Fuck! Son of a Bitch!"

(37)
I guess I forgot...
To set emergency brakes.
They lock the rear wheels.

(38)
Don't forget that brake!
In some cars, it's a pedal,
Left of the dashboard.

(39)
You press the pedal,
To lock the rear wheels in place,
In emergencies.

(40)
There is a lever,
Located under the dash.
You pull to release.

(41)
Some are different.
You PULL a lever to lock.
Then, push to release.

(42)
I pulled the lever,
In between the two front seats,
To set the e-brake.

(43)
I guess I'm lucky,
That I did not get injured.
Next time, I'll use it.

(44)
I pulled the jack out.
And, I lowered it again.
I re-attached it.

(45)
I started over.
Turn it right to raise the car,
And, left to lower.

(46)
I lifted the spare.
"Where did I put those damn nuts?"
Always… keep them safe.

(47)
I remembered soon,
They were in my front pocket.
Soon, It's almost done!

(48)
I lifted the spare,
Pushed the holes over the bolts.
Then, I screwed the nuts.

(49)
Using jack handle,
Right for tight, left for loose,
I turned the nuts right.

(50)
Nut goes on the bolt.
Spin it around until tight.
Put the round side in.

(51)
Go in a circle.
Tighten one nut, then skip one.
Tighten all the nuts.

(52)
Now… I'm almost done.
Turn the jack left to lower.
Then, remove the jack.

(53)
Just when I was done,
A car came by to give help.
"Thank you, I'm all done!"

(54)
I put jack in trunk.
I put the blown tire there too.
Don't forget hubcap.

(55)
I shined the flashlight,
Looked for parts, and tools, and stuff,
And, cleaned myself off.

(56)
I lit my cigar.
I was grateful that people…
Offered to help out.

(57)
I was most grateful,
There was not ten pounds of pot,
Hidden in the trunk.

(58)
And, that's the story;
That's how I started on my…

HAIKU HOLIDAY!

Jason Flick

INTERNET HOOKEY

Yeah! I am really excited to be home. I am very excited to be starting my "Haiku Holiday." So, to celebrate, I'm going to skip class; skip internet class that is. It's okay, I think I have it all wrapped up. I should be getting an A, and tonight's the last assignment. I don't think I need it. God bless the internet. Now, I'm going to enjoy some pursuit of happiness by enjoying some delicious microwave movie butter popcorn, and, a delicious beer to start the Haiku Holiday.

PURSUIT OF HAPPINESS

I guess I forgot to tell you, I'm unemployed. Also, I'm on probation. But, the good news is that I am almost finished with my probation. Since my probation, I have become more interested in government and laws and stuff. Ergo, I thought I would take a moment to consider… The Declaration of Independence.

"We hold these truths to be self-evident [This is what we believe is logical common sense], That all men are created equal [we all come from sperm and a vagina], and they are endowed by their creator with certain unalienable rights [God is our creator, we have free will], that among these are life [The government can't take our life], liberty [the government can't take our freedom], and the PURSUIT OF HAPPINESS [We should be able to follow free market ideals and make personal choices to do what we want]- That to secure these rights, governments are instituted among men [government is created by man to protect these rights], deriving their just powers from the consent of the governed [The government needs permission from the people it manages], that whenever any form of government becomes destructive of these ends, it is the right of the people to alter or abolish it [When the government gets pissy, people have the right to make a new one], and to institute new government, laying its foundation on such principles [a new government can be made, as long as it serves the people]. And organizing its powers into such form, as to them shall seem most likely to affect their safety and HAPPINESS."

Haiku Holiday

If this is the declaration of independence, how come I'm not happy, and how come I have to pay taxes, and why are people in jail, and why did they have slaves?

First, this is only the most famous part of the Declaration of Independence. This is only one paragraph, and there's like another three pages. Second, the Declaration of Independence was just a blueprint, for the government, and a reason for war. It was not legally binding, because there was no independent government yet. Third, we have to pay taxes because the government has been established where we have representation and the right to vote. We need to pay taxes to do our share to pay for the government that protects public safety and society. Fourth, people are in jail because they committed a crime, and were found guilty in a court of law. People are not supposed to be put in jail because of what they say, or believe, or because someone does not like them and pays to put them there. Fifth, there were slaves because this document was not the real government, yet it explained the philosophy and goals of the government. The new government was based on representation and compromise. The North gave freedom to slaves, but the South maintained slavery.

The ACTUAL United States Government, was created under the rules of the Constitution of the United States, that provided for the democratic right to vote for representatives, and for changes to the constitutional laws. In the beginning, only white male property owners could vote. But as time progressed, slaves were freed and all men were granted the right to vote. Then, women were granted the right to vote. You do not have to own property, but you have to be 18, and a citizen.

This was a contract among Americans, that they agreed they did not want to serve Britain, and have a king, and they were agreeing to fight a war to create a democracy. It was based on John Locke's Social Contract, and Thomas Payne's Common Sense. The important thing that I want to talk about is… The Pursuit of Happiness.

Although when these individuals stated, the pursuit of happiness, they were largely concerned with the right to private property, and a free market economy that the king could not take from them, for me today, it is about the right to drink beer and eat microwave popcorn.

#7: HAPPINESS: THE PURSUIT OF BEER AND POPCORN

(1)
A delicious treat;
Beer, and microwave popcorn.
Like salt, and pepper.

(2)
Microwave popcorn,
Is God's secret gift to man.
A cheap and fast meal.

(3)
When in welding school,
Students were from Africa.
I showed them popcorn.

(4)
They were so happy.
It was so cheap and easy.
It made a whole meal.

(5)
I tried to explain.
If you eat too much popcorn,
Then it's hard to poop.

(6)
Microwave popcorn,
Is great with a cold beer too.
But, don't drink and weld.

(7)
Today, I'm drinking,
Busch Signature Copper Beer.
The can's copper orange.

(8)
And, so is the beer.
It's a red dark brown color.
It tastes like rye bread.

(9)
Any beer is good,
When with microwave popcorn.
That's today's pursuit.

#8: LIFE AND DEATH: ALL THE WORLD'S A STAGE

(1)
I enjoy t.v.
I enjoy late night t.v.;
Movie stars and news.

(2)
News is serious.
It's on later than the news.
They talk about sex.

(3)
Sex and beer and drugs,
Are all on late night t.v.,
And, some music too.

(4)
Magicians are cool.
Hollywood starlets are great;
Comedians too.

(5)
Ed Sullivan Show,
Was where the Beatles played first.
Elvis was there too.

(6)
There was Jack Benny.
He had Nat King Cole, and child,
When Jazz was… "the thing."

(7)
There was Jack Parr too.
Before, Elvis was made King.
Don't forget Bob Hope.

(8)
Bob Hope was… "The Dope."
He had writers write the jokes.
I didn't know this.

(9)
How's he so funny?
I guess they all have some help.
It's still fun to watch.

(10)
Then came the 60's.
Dick Cavett took the front page,
When John Lennon showed.

(11)
The funniest man,
Was a mystery comic;
His name… Lenny Bruce.

(12)
Also of the greats,
Was a comedy duo;
The Smothers Brothers.

(13)
Don't know why or where,
But, somehow they broke the rules,
And… they got fired!

(14)
Then, Johnny Carson,
Started late night t.v. shows,
With Ed McMahon too.

(15)
And, he had a band.
It was a swing jazz band with...
Doc Severenson.

(16)
David Letterman,
Started late late night t.v.,
With lots of high jinks.

(17)
Jay Leno appeared,
And took over Johnny's place.
Letterman was pissed!

(18)
David moved his show,
To after news... CBS,
To compete with Jay.

(19)
Late night t.v. wars,
Is what they called this big change.
His old show was gone.

(20)
Conan O'Brien,
Took over Late late tv;
David's old late show.

(21)
Conan had a band,
Called the Max Weinberg Seven,
And... Andy Richter.

(22)
Today there's new shows.
There's the Jimmy Kimmel Live.
That's on ABC.

(23)
There's the late, late show.
That's the latest late night show,
With Carson Daly.

(24)
There's Craig Fergusson,
After David Letterman,
The CBS last.

(25)
Another war passed,
When Jay Leno left his show.
Another torch passed.

(26)
This was tragedy.
Conan O'Brien moved there.
From late late, to… late.

(27)
He replaced Jay's spot.
From N.Y.C. to L.A.
But then… Jay came back!

(28)
He added a spot.
Jay Leno went on prime time.
Then, it was a war!

(29)
Conan got cancelled!
And, Jay took back his old spot.
Conan… went cable.

(30)
Jimmy Fallon Show,
Had taken Conan's old spot;
Fallon, in New York.

(31)
That was a big war.
Then, there was peace for awhile;
At least, a few years.

(32)
Until… Leno Quit.
Then, it started all over.
Fallon took Jay's place.

(33)
But, he moved the show!;
From L.A.…. to NYC!;
Reverse of Conan.

(34)
Now, Jimmy Fallon…
Is on top for NBC.
Who took his place then?

(35)
The new kid in town;
Seth Meyers from SNL…
(Saturday Night Live!)

(36)
That's today's lineup.
There's a few stars that I missed;
Arsenio Hall.

(37)
Arsenio, first…
African American.
Left, but then… came back.

(38)
There was Seinfeld's guy.
He was the Spike Feresten Show.
Still, no female show.

(39)
Ladies host A.M.
That's a whole different subject.
There's a point to this.

(40)
Life and Death t.v.;
Here today, gone tomorrow.
When you're hot, you're hot!

(41)
When you're not... you're not.
It was Shakespeare that warned us,
"All the world's a stage."

(42)
Mortality will...
Touch everyone at some time.
There is a lesson.

(43)
Yes, shine while you can.
But, you should have more in life,
Than just the spotlight.

(44)
We're all on t.v.
Some shine at work, some at play.
Everyone's special.

(45)
But, one should have more,
To fill in their time of life,
Than... late night t.v.

Haiku Holiday

BIG DEAL: Oops. Writing haikus is hard because it is hard to fit in the words. So I didn't get the late night tv names exactly right, and I left out some of the bands, and I left out a couple of historical shows. "Whateves People." Alphabetically from ABC, CBS, to NBC, I will list the correct names of the shows, and their bands. I thank the late night tv shows for keeping me company and informed. I will have to get a job soon, so I will probably have to cut back late night tv... and cigars.

ABC: Jimmy Kimmel Live, Cleto and the Cletones.
CBS: Late Show with David Letterman, Paul Shaffer and the CBS Orchestra
(formerly Late Night with David Letterman, on NBC. Letterman has announced intention to retire, to be replaced by Stephen Colbert.
The Late Late Show with Craig Ferguson.
The Arsenio Hall Show (Distributed by CBS)
NBC: The Tonight Show with Jay Leno, Branford Marsalis, Kevin Eubanks, Rickey Minor.
Then, The Jay Leno Show
Late Night with Conan O'Brien, with Andy Richter, and The Max Weinberg Seven.
Then, The Tonight Show with Conan O' Brien. Then, Conan, on TBS with Jimmy Vivino and The Basic Cable Band.
Late Night with Jimmy Fallon, with Steve Higgins, and The Roots.,
Then,
The Tonight Show Starring Jimmy Fallon.
Late Night with Seth Meyers, The 8G Band with Fred Armisen
Last Call with Carson Daly.

DAY ONE: THURSDAY

LIT LADY

Haiku Holiday

#9: BEAUTY: BOUNCING BETTY PAGE

(1)
What is beautiful?
Beauty is different for all;
Cultural values.

(2)
Beauty's a campfire,
As it dances with brilliance,
Or, smoke acending.

(3)
Beauty is the stars,
Holes in the curtain of night,
Giving mystery.

(4)
Beauty is the snow.
Every snowflake is unique,
Like paint from the sky.

(5)
Beauty is in rain;
Tapping on windows,
Angelic phone calls.

(6)
Beauty is in grass;
Like a soft ocean of green,
Filling a golf course.

(7)
Beauty is in clouds.
Like floating cartoon pillows;
Animal Crackers.

(8)
Beauty's in cities.
Buildings like concrete rulers;
Lines pointing to God.

(9)
Earth, Wind, Fire, Water;
They give us inspiration;
As food for the soul.

(10)
Beauty's in the soul.
The origin of language.
Poetic fountain.

(11)
The soul's our life source.
The soul makes us who we are.
The soul provides love.

(12)
Bouncing Betty Page,
Dancing Diva of Burlesque,
Loves… to stir the soul.

#10: ART: SMART ART

(1)
The 1950's
Invented 3D movies,
With 3D Glasses.

(2)
3D is short for,
3 Dimensional Glasses;
One eye red, one blue.

(3)
The left eye is red.
The right eye is blue color.
They don't use them now.

(4)
New Technology,
Has replaced the red, blue scene.
You can still get them.

(5)
Find them at toy stores.
You can get them at art stores.
Don't wear them too much.

(6)
They could ruin eyes.
I think your eyes would change back.
But this, I don't know.

(7)
You can wear them safe.
They're okay for a few hours.
They make films look real.

(8)
Only, 3D kind.
Here's how they made the movies.
I guess this is how.

(9)
They use two colors,
Obviously, red and blue.
They make one print RED.

(10)
Then, make one print… BLUE!
Then they put them together,
Or, show side by side.

(11)
They make things look wild.
Even if they're not 3D;
Magnify colors.

(12)
Not truly better,
But, an altered perception;
Artificial drugs.

(13)
I had a crush on gal.
A hot Irish lesbian.
She was a shop clerk.

(14)
Worked at the museum.
I would go there everyday.
I was writing book.

(15)
It was an art book.
About a famous painting.
We would talk a lot.

(16)
The Painting was called,
Red Haired Girl, 1919
From Emil Nolde

(17)
I would buy stuff there,
Just so I could talk to her.
We talked about art.

(18)
She was art student.
She was very smart and sweet.
We didn't go out.

Haiku Holiday

(19)
I was just kidding.
She may not have been… lesbo.
But, I stopped going.

(20)
I was on probie;
Wasn't supposed to be there.
She…was dating guard.

(21)
He visited too.
Smithwick's imported Irish;
It's made by Guinness.

(22)
I picked up bottle.
The label's shiny blood red.
I drink, and I think…

(23)
Of Irish red head.
She was a brilliant young RED,
And, she left me BLUE.

(24)
I stopped going there.
I thought the painting haunted,
And, I stopped writing.

(25)
Fire's cool in 3D,
Watching TV in 3D,
3D Beer's the best.

(26)
So, I still like art.
I still wear 3D Glasses.
But, not while driving.

(27)
I went back one time.
The painting was still displayed.
But, she was not found.

There are a lot of great art museum websites where you can view paintings with 3D glasses on the internet. Here is a list of my favorite paintings (in random order) to view with red and blue 3D glasses that I saw at The Art Institute of Chicago:

Paul Delvaux, The Awakening of the Forest, 1939
Jackson Pollock, 289B, and 299A
Rene Magritte, The Banquet, 1958
Conrad Felixmuller, The Death of the Poet Rheiner, 1925
Joan Miro, Juanita Obrador, 1918
Amedeo Modigliani, Jacques and Berthe Lipchitz, 1916
Paul Cezanne, Harlequin, 1889
Pablo Picasso, The Old Guitarist, 1903
Claude Monet, Water Lillies, 1906
Maurice de Vlaminck, House at Chateau, 1945
And…
Emil Nolde, Red Haired Girl, 1919

#11: LOVE: HAIKU HEAVEN

(1)
How to pick up chicks,
By using haikus to flirt.
First, find a hot girl.

(2)
Next, check for a ring.
Then, watch out for her boyfriend.
Then… take off your clothes.

(3)
Then, write a haiku.
I was joking… don't get nude.
Here's a sample.

(4)
Hi Lou, How are You?
I tell you what I will do;
Write a poem for you.

(5)
If you have the will.
Write it on her hand with pen.
But, good luck with that.

(6)
Well, guess what ladies?
You can try this on guys too.
Men like it… sexy.

(7)
If you get married,
And, you met from a haiku,
Name your child, Jason.

(8)
That's a cool story.
How you met from a haiku,
And, got the name here.

(9)
Good luck, and be safe.
One more important idea,
Don't forget breath mints.

#12: MATTER: A BAD EXAMPLE

(1)
A bad example,
Is the following haiku.
Here's what NOT to do.

(2)
I like your big boobs!
I think they're really quite big.
I bet… they taste great!

(3)
"What? It's a haiku!
Oh, Come on, I'm just joking.
But, I bet they do!"

(4)
It's all in timing.
Some women like to trash talk.
Do it with a wink.

(5)
Are boobs not your thing?
Here's something else you can try…
Booty compliments!

(6)
I like your hot ass!
You must work out… like, a lot!
I have a quarter!

(7)
I almost forgot.
It would also really help…
If you're both real drunk!

#13: WEALTH: TRASH OR TREASURE

(1)
They say trash for one,
Is treasure for another.
We have different views.

(2)
One thing that I know,
Friendship is the best treasure,
Even when... trashy.

(3)
Another treasure,
Is ice cold beer when you're hot.
It's like fluid gold.

(4)
Social lubricant;
Fluid gold can help make friends,
Or, make you lose them.

(5)
25 ounces;
Budweiser, "The King of Beers.";
With one extra ounce!

(6)
Harvard Let's Go Guide,
Says the original Bud,
Is Bohemian.

(7)
That means it is brewed,
In Czechslovakia.
Somewhere nearby Prague.

(8)
I like mine… with head.
In Brazil, it's called "spuma."
That's a crown of foam.

(9)
Spin the empty can.
A metal ballerina,
It will dance and sway.

(10)
Best, in a glass mug;
Ice cold and covered in frost;
Clear amber nectar.

(11)
Hops, rice, barley malt,
Make a protein filled beverage.
And, beer is fat free!

(12)
Man's best friend is God.
Man's second best friend is Dog.
Man's third best friend… Beer.

(13)
Sometimes the best wealth,
Is a glass of fluid gold,
And a friend to share.

#14: LAW: HAIKU TEN COMMANDMENTS

(1)
The Bible has laws.
The 10 Commandments are laws.
These were the first ones.

Haiku Holiday

(2)
A law is a rule.
Jesus said, "follow these rules."
Here's simple version.

(3)
The real ones are found,
In the Bible; Exodus;
Deuteronomy.

(4)
Here's the haiku list.
The First Commandment says to:
Worship the one God.

(5)
This is the real God.
The Second Commandment says:
Don't worship false gods.

(6)
Don't worship idols.
The Third Commandment says that:
Don't curse with God's name.

(7)
Show respect to God.
The Fourth Commandment says that:
Sunday is holy.

(8)
Jews do it different.
For Jews it's on Saturday.
God's day, once a week.

(9)
Go to church, and rest.
The Fifth Commandment says to:
Love your Mom and Dad.

(10)
Do what they tell you.
The Sixth Commandment tells you:
Do not kill people.

(11)
Even, when angry.
The Seventh Commandment says:
Don't cheat on your wife.

(12)
Don't cheat on your husband.
The Eighth Commandment tells us:
We're not to steal things.

(13)
Don't Xerox good books.
The Ninth Commandment tells us,
Don't lie and gossip.

(14)
Even on "Face Book."
The Tenth Commandment tells us,
Do not be jealous…

(15)
Of, your neighbor's stuff,
Or, of his hot sexy wife.
Those are the first laws.

(16)
There are many more.
Don't have sex with animals.
Jesus explains them.

(17)
I'm the Son of God.
I'm here to teach and forgive.
There's only one God.

(18)
But, 3 parts to God.
He's a Holy Trinity.
There's God the Father;

(19)
The Holy Spirit;
And, God the Son; messenger.
Obey holy laws.

(20)
Two most important;
You should love and worship God.
And, Love your neighbor.

(21)
When you break a law,
Or, when you make a mistake,
Then, pray to Jesus.

(22)
Say you are sorry.
Ask Jesus to Forgive you.
Jesus will save you.

(23)
Jesus promises;
My Grace is sufficient for you;
The New Testament.

#15: STATE: THE GRIFTY FIFTY

(1)
American Flag,
Has 50 stars for the states;
50 stars, and states.

(2)
A Federation;
Every state is different,
All… American.

(3)
The United States;
All different, but one country.
There was civil war.

(4)
1861
Until 1865.
North versus the South.

(5)
North were the Yankees.
South were the Confederates.
South tried to start new.

(6)
This was a BIG war.
The biggest war in U.S,
Remained… one country.

(7)
2 new rebel states;
Washington, Colorado.
They legalized pot.

(8)
Some states have no tax;
Nevada and Florida,
Have no income tax.

(9)
One of my favorites,
Is the land of cheese and beer;
State of Wisconsin.

(10)
Home to the great beer…
It's one of my favorite beers,
Pabst Blue Ribbon Beer.

(11)
The Can's Red, White, Blue.
Brewed since 1844,
Before Civil War.

(12)
Made in Milwaukee,
P.B.R.A.S.A.P.
24 ounces.

(13)
I want to find state,
That will legalize Cubans…
FREE CUBAN STOGIES!

#16: MEMORY: CLASS OF 99

(1)
Some say that beer is great!
And, some say that sex… is fine!
Class of… 99!

(2)
Mexico is great!
The drinking age is 18!
But, nobody cares.

(3)
Canada… kicks ass!
The drinking age is 18!
Or, so I have heard.

(4)
It doesn't make sense.
Smoke, drive, vote, and be drafted…
But, don't try to drink!

(5)
Not just high school kids,
But what about college kids?
It… makes a challenge.

(6)
I drank in high school.
I also drank in college.
It just causes stress.

(7)
Brazil is backwards!
You can drink when you're 16!
Don't drive… til 18!

(8)
Still, driving is good.
I got to drive at 16!
That was amazing.

(9)
There's one famous beer,
That college kids drink a lot.
It's easy and cheap.

(10)
That's Miller Lite Beer!
It's a red, white, and blue can.
It's a pilsner beer.

(11)
It's what most people…
Think of, when they think of beer.
Because of college.

(12)
Or… back in high school.
The taste brings back memories.
Drinking in the park.

(13)
I don't remember,
How, or where, we would get it?
Friends with big brothers.

(14)
Borrowed from parents?
Or, using a fake I.D.
I guess it won't change.

(15)
Special occasions;
We would not drink every day.
We were A students.

(16)
Trying to be old.
Now, I try to be younger.
Beer can make memories.

#17: LIBERTY/FREEDOM: PROHIBITION BEER

(1)
Colorado's Coors
Coors Lite's in a silver can.
It scares away wolves.

(2)
Twenty four ounces;
It's called the silver bullet,
Because it's fast?

(3)
It's a special can.
When cold, the mountains turn blue;
Cold like a mountain.

(4)
It was work to find.
Prohibition is alive.
No beer after ten.

(5)
I stopped at the store
"Sorry sir, No beer past ten."
What? You're kidding me?

(6)
I did not know that!
I live in a rural town.
Looks… like a road trip.

(7)
There's another town.
It's eight miles away from here.
I hope it's open.

(8)
It's past ten o clock.
And, now it's dark and raining.
I hope they're open.

(9)
I will miss my show.
But I hear a beer calling.
It's saying my name.

(10)
Windshield wipers on.
It sounds like they are talking.
I tell them, "Shut Up!"

Haiku Holiday

(11)
Turn on radio.
It's time for 80's music.
It's a "Safety Dance."

(12)
The lights are still on.
They close in 15 minutes.
Made it just in time.

(13)
Hey do you sell beer?
Yeah, it's over in the back.
Can I still buy some?

(14)
Yes, You can buy some.
What kind of beer should I get?
It's a Coors Lite Nite!

(15)
Then it stopped raining.
Say, goodnight windshield wipers.
I'm on my way home.

(16)
Now I sit in awe,
In front of a silver can,
That changes color.

(17)
I open the can,
And pour honey colored brew,
In my cold glass mug.

(18)
I open a bag,
Of classic saltine crackers,
And dip them in beer.

(19)
A great late night snack.
Saltine crackers and cold beer;
Time to say... good night.

GREEN MILL PROHIBITION POETRY SLAM

I forgot what I wanted to say. But, anyway, what is a speakeasy? A speakeasy takes its roots from during 1920's America, or "The Roaring 20's", or "The Jazz Age." It was the era of Prohibition. Prohibition occurred after World War I, and alcohol became illegal in the United States, except with a prescription from a doctor. And, a lot of people still wanted to drink and party. People would pay through the nose for "illegal" alcohol. People would have private parties at bars and restaurants where they could drink "illegal" alcohol. This was called a "speakeasy," because it was a secret, and you had to know a password to get in. Basically, a speakeasy was an "underground" bar.

There's a famous landmark in Chicago. I don't think it's a big deal. It's been on television, and in movies, and things like that. It's an authentic speakeasy from the 1920's, and it's very glamorous and elegant. It's historically preserved. It's called The Green Mill Café, or The Green Mill. It's on the North Side of Chicago. It's famed for being a former speakeasy. But, it really stands out, so I don't know how it was a speakeasy.

It's a very beautiful jazz lounge with big luxurious booths, and 1920's paintings on the wall. It must have been a restaurant, and then they would close down at night, or maybe they had a secret back room. Supposedly, it has escape tunnels behind the bar. Maybe they just stored and imported their beer and liquor in the tunnels. I won't tell you where it is, but you can find it. It's a popular place.

These days, on Sunday nights, they host a "slam" poetry night. This is in the tradition of the 1950's Jack Kerouac Beatnik Poets. The beatnik poets would improvise poetry and snap their fingers because they were on speed or dope. This was called "stream of consciousness" poetry.

Haiku Holiday

The beatniks would host poetry readings at the San Francisco, City Lights Book Store.

Jack Kerouac, Alan Ginsburg, William Burroughs, and later Bob Dylan, and Joan Baez were some of the bohemian beatnik icons. They still do these "poetry slam" dramatic interpretation poetry readings on Sunday nights at The Green Mill, in Chicago. It's very popular, and it gets very crowded. Sometimes people will read poetry, sometimes they will improvise, and sometimes they will have music and contests. One time, I signed up to be a reader, but I didn't make it that far. Instead, here is a poetic interpretation of what may, or may not, have happened.

#18: VIOLENCE: GREEN MILL GIRL POETRY SLAM

(1)
It's now one A.M.
It's chilly, and rainy out.
Good for memories.

(2)
I sit here quiet.
I listen to the raindrops.
And I drink a beer.

(3)
This is a new beer.
It's from Miller Brewing Co.
I hope they keep it.

(4)
It's high quality.
It came from the gas station.
But, it's premium.

(5)
The can is dark grey.
With a spade from playing cards.
It has a red M!

(6)
It's golden lager.
It has a walnut color.
And, it's called… Fortune.

(7)
It's a special treat,
With 6.9 alcohol,
And micro-brew taste.

(8)
Spades are the army.
Diamonds are for the merchants.
Hearts are for the church.

(9)
Clubs are for labor.
They're all used for playing cards.
All society.

(10)
Which suite is for you?
They all like to drink some beer.
Which one's for poets?

(11)
Here's a great story,
About poetry, and love.
And, some violence.

(12)
From poetry night,
At the Green Mill, Chicago.
It was a while back.

(13)
How I fell in love,
And, broke up with my dream girl,
All in the same night.

Haiku Holiday

(14)
A smile, and a wink;
She stole my heart with a look,
From across the room.

(15)
One went left, One right.
Who's drink's this? I think I know.
She chose, the stiff one.

(16)
Drinks are on the house!
Who said that? That is NOT true!
Who's going to pay?

(17)
Hey, That's MY girlfriend!
She is NOT available.
Well, that's what YOU think.

(18)
Fuck you very much!
Fuck me? No, I say Fuck You!
I'll see you outside!

(19)
Bing, Bang, Boom, I'm out.
It sucks to be on probie.
That means, probation.

(20)
No, I didn't fight.
I snuck out in a hurry.
I kissed a street curb.

Some interesting notes. There is a reference in this previous poem to Robert Frost's, "Whose Woods these are? I think I know." Also, alcohol is no longer prohibited in America for people over the age of 21, but, there are still speakeasy's today. There are secret last minute

59

Jason Flick

"raves" for techno dance parties held in warehouses and abandoned buildings. Also, there are speakeasy private parties and bars. Some are for fun, or fundraisers. Some are for privacy, like a private unmarked and secret bar for celebrities, or politicians. Some, are for selling tax-free liquor. And, some are for recreational vices like illegal drugs, gambling, and prostitution. And some…
Are all of these. They still exist in big cities.

One last note of interest; according to David Biggs' book, *Cocktails*, one benefit from prohibition was that it gave birth to the modern cocktail.

"Whatever their origin, cocktails came into their own during the American Prohibition years of 1920s and 30s. Illicit "moonshine" stills often produced liquor of very dubious quality, and these concoctions sometimes needed all the help they could get, to make them palatable. This led to a wide range of interesting mixtures, some of which (like the Martini and the Manhattan) earned immortality as classic cocktails.

When Prohibition was repealed in 1933, the standard of liquor improved enormously, but cocktails had come to stay as an essential part of sophisticated life."

#19: JUSTICE: JUST ICE BEER

(1)
Milwaukee's Best Ice.
Milwaukee's Best is classic.
It's a bargain beer.

(2)
This can's from gas stop.
Milwaukee's Best Ice; ice brewed;
5.9 percent.

Haiku Holiday

(3)
It's a shiny gold.
The can is blue, white, and gold.
These are cop colors.

(4)
It's both sweet and tart.
It's smooth and easy to drink.
With lots of bubbles.

(5)
This is not just ice.
This poems about justice;
What to do when stopped.

(6)
God bless the police.
They really serve and protect.
Risk their lives for good.

(7)
If you are driving,
And get pulled over by cops,
Here is what to do.

(8)
You must have papers.
You need a driver's license,
And car insurance.

(9)
You need license plates.
They must have current stickers,
And, registration.

(10)
Prepare your papers.
If you are really quite poor,
Get the minimum.

(11)
If you own your car,
To get an insurance card…
Liability.

(12)
Put papers in car.
Registration, insurance…
Put in the glove box.

(13)
When you're pulled over,
Just pull over right away,
No matter where at.

(14)
They don't like to wait.
Then, turn on your inside lights.
Roll down your window.

(15)
If you have something,
That you are not supposed to,
Put it out of view.

(16)
Put your hands on wheel.
Then, wait for them to approach.
I have a bond card.

(17)
If you get ticket,
They will want to keep license,
Until you pay it.

(18)
Your auto club card,
Might substitute for license,
If you get ticket.

Haiku Holiday

(19)
Be sure to stay calm.
They are just doing their job.
And, they risk their lives.

(20)
Try and be polite.
Just say, "Hello officer."
"How can I help you?"

(21)
They will want papers.
Tell them, "They're in the glove box."
"I need to get them."

(22)
Before you get them,
Tell them about your bond card.
Ask if they'll take it.

(23)
Be sure to ask now.
Otherwise, you will forget.
Then, give with license.

(24)
Don't admit your guilt.
You're innocent until proof.
You can go to court.

(25)
Before giving docs,
Apologize for mistakes,
And, ask for warning.

(26)
Give honest reason.
"Sorry for any mistakes."
"I don't know this road."

(27)
"I'm laid off right now,"
"And, I'm on a tight budget."
"Can I have warning?"

(28)
Be sure to say please.
You must ask before you give...
Them your documents.

(29)
That's all you can do.
If you're nice, they might do it.
Don't argue and fight.

(30)
If they give ticket,
Just be grateful that you drive.
You might be guilty.

(31)
You can try to fight,
If you want to go to court.
That's another tale.

(32)
If you get ticket,
You should still say "Thank you sir."
They might save your life.

(33)
Here's a fun beer treat.
It's cold beer with hot bacon.
Here's the recipe.

(34)
First, take an aspirin.
This will prevent heart attack.
Bacon and beer's good.

Haiku Holiday

(35)
Take one strip bacon.
Then put it in microwave.
Cook for two minutes.

(36)
Cut it in pieces.
Add it to a glass of beer.
Let it sit and cool.

(37)
It smells delicious.
It tastes creamy and salty.
Beer and bacon's good!

(38)
It's bacon and beer.
It's the breakfast of winners,
Or... lunch and dinner.

(39)
Oh, there's one more thing.
You should try and drive safely,
And, follow the rules.

Post script: You can also use dried salad bacon topping.

EMERGENCY MEDITATION

Sometimes I get really, really, angry. Maybe my boss dumps on me to make himself feel powerful. Maybe a friend makes fun of me, or betrays me. Maybe I'm really proud of an accomplishment, but someone else belittles it, or, they make fun of it, or, they try to undermine it. Maybe I'm in love with a woman, and she loves someone else. Maybe I think my girlfriend is cheating on me. Or, maybe it's that time of month and she picks a fight, and yells at me. Or maybe she flirts with someone else... or she IS cheating on me. Maybe I forget to pay a bill, and the credit card company adds a late fee. Maybe I think my electric bill is too high, and there's nothing I can do about it. Maybe I find the perfect house, and then get turned down for a loan, or someone else buys it. Maybe I just failed a class after putting in a lot of work and studying. Maybe my car won't start for no reason, or I get a flat tire, and I don't want to have to buy a new tire. Maybe I'm at the grocery store and I go to buy something, and the price was marked wrong. Maybe I get to the bank just as they're closing. Or, maybe I just get a fucking ticket… (even though I probably was speeding and deserve it.)

This is not in the bible, but here's what I do to clear my mind and calm down. Most of the time, it's pride that makes me angry. Pride is good. It motivates us, and inspires us. But, it can also really hurt, and cause us to make mistakes. I do a meditation. I do this silently to myself, but one should be alone. You can go into the bathroom, and sit on the toilet, or you can do it in your car.

This is very simple. I just close my eyes, and repeat these words over and over (maybe 20 times).

"Praise God. Jesus have mercy."

Then, while I'm thinking these words, I try to remember happy times, and things I'm grateful for. I try to remember that other people suffer, and have suffered much worse things.
I try to think of the pain and humiliation of Jesus on the Cross. I try to remember that God loves me. I try to remember that things could be a lot worse for me. Then, the pain and anger goes away, and I feel better. Maybe I'm still upset, but not as much. Then, I try to think of good things that result. Maybe I can solve the problem later, or something good will happen that will make up for this problem.

"You goddamn mutherfucking cock sucking suns of bitches. I will never ever ever pay you. I hope you burn in hell forever you stupid rotten scumbag assholes!"

Oops, I should not have said that. They're not going to give me a payment plan now. Damn it, I need to get my water turned back on.

Haiku Holiday

Good things: I guess it's time to find a new apartment. My landlord's a jerk anyway.
I guess there could be a lot worse things that I could be doing. I could be in combat, or in the hospital, or in jail, or a homeless beggar. I think there's a good tv show on later. Maybe I could have a cigar, or go for a walk.

DAY TWO: FRIDAY

HAPPY HARRY

I FAILED, NO YOU FAILED!

"Goddam you to hell! You're a liar! You're a lying wicked witch! You're a fake! You're a goddamn phony!"

Oops. I found out today... I failed my class. It turns out that last internet class that I skipped, was mandatory. I failed the class that I worked so hard on; the class that I needed an A in to continue my studies. Not only did I not get an A... I failed. I fucking failed.

The teacher is a real bitch. A real mean witch. Well, it's not a big surprise. I tried to be reasonable on the phone. I tried really hard not to get angry, and to listen. Near the end of our conversation... I lost it. I called her "a Goddamn liar", and said "Goddamn you to hell! I said this because... she's really religious.

She's really religious, but, she's still a bitch. I guess there's a place for her in heaven.
I pray to God, I don't have to be near her. Or, my heaven... will be a hell. Here's the thing, I'm religious too. So, what happens when two religious people hate each other?

Jesus says to try not to do that (hate people). Jesus says, don't use the Lord's name in vain (which means, don't say "Goddamnit.) Here's what I'm going to do. I'm going to pray to Jesus to forgive me for losing my temper and shouting on the phone and insulting and cursing the shit out of that evil woman. Oh yes, and I need forgiveness for the half dozen irate messages that I left. I wanted to get my $2000 worth out of that class.

Now, I am very worried and upset. I still have to go to court mandated anger management class. I have to sit through some dumb questions, and be humiliated and made to feel stupid. And, now that I failed my class, I have to find a job. And, I might even get evicted.
The Irish girl from the store turned me down for a date. I was really hoping I might get her to marry me... for citizenship and stuff. I am getting older everyday. And, I'm afraid the police are following me, and want to put me back in jail.

#20: EMOTION: SEX PISTOLS AND ANGER MANAGEMENT

(1)
There was a great band.
They were called, The Sex Pistols.
Johnny Rotten Sang.

(2)
John Lydon's his name.
And, Sid Vicious played the base.
Later, they broke up.

(3)
Sid, then died from drugs.
Public Image Limited,
Was John's new rock band.

(4)
One of their songs says,
"Anger is an energy."
Perhaps this is true.

(5)
But, you should beware.
Anger will cause great damage.
You can make mistakes.

(6)
Jesus gives warning.
I call this, "quick, slow, slower."
It sounds like sex guide.

(7)
Be quick to listen.
Then, be slow to get angry.
Slower to respond.

Haiku Holiday

(8)
This is biblical;
Anger management training.
Be quick, slow, slower!

#21: EQUALITY: RAINBOW BEER

(1)
It's Old Milwaukee
Only a dollar and nine,
It's called a "Tall Boy".

(2)
Gas station beer rocks.
It's cold and ready to drink.
But don't drink and drive.

(3)
Please don't drink and drive.
But, you can drink a little.
Not at the same time.

(4)
Jelly Beans and Beer!
With one box of jelly beans,
Beer is a rainbow.

(5)
Like America,
Is a rainbow of cultures.
Living side by side.

(6)
All over the World,
They come to America,
For freedom… and beer!

(7)
Sure, there's rich and poor.
But, we can all be voters.
Just don't... drink and vote!

(8)
Jelly Beans and beer,
Is like American blood...
All mixed together.

(9)
It's called rainbow beer.
Like drinking liquid candy,
It helps get you stiff.

(10)
Joseph Schlitz Brewing
It's made in America
Also called, Old M.

(11)
It's Old Milwaukee
24 ounces of beer...
Made in Milwaukee.

(12)
One rule when you pour,
Tilt the glass to avoid foam,
And use a clear glass.

(13)
It's like liquid sun.
I drink it with a cigar.
That's another tale.

Haiku Holiday

#22: HABIT: FREUD'S FROLIC

(1)
According to Freud,
Sometimes a cigar is just…
And, just a cigar!

#23: WISDOM: SHINING MOON

(1)
Hey, It's Friday Night.
I have a Spanish cigar,
And, a quart of beer.

(2)
It's Miller High Life;
One Quarter of a GALLON!
32 Ounces.

(3)
But, I am at home!
I can only fight… myself.
Or, throw up… on me.

(4)
It's called… "beer champagne".
Tonight, It's a champagne glass…
With, the red lady.

(5)
She sits in the moon;
High in the sky, with red boots.
She gives me a toast!

(6)
It's from Milwaukee;
Home of Harley Davidson;
That's in Wisconsin!

(7)
It's a late night treat...
With, peanut butter cookies!
Don't use milk... use beer.

(8)
I dip them in suds.
The foam, is kind of like milk.
I leave one floating.

(9)
Sausage, beer, and bikes;
That's what makes Milwaukee good...
And, lots of cheese curds.

(10)
The High Life Quart Can...
Is a really giant can.
But, it gives a buzz.

(11)
Cookies and beer WIN!
It's true, it may be a sin.
It makes your head... spin.

(12)
Which, might help you win,
When you flash, a silly grin,
To... Anais Niin.

(13)
A Spanish cigar,
Helps make it all go down slow,
And, leaves a warm glow.

DAY THREE: SATURDAY

FUNNY HAT MAN

#24: REASONING: HAIKU PHILOSOPHE

(1)
I think... thus I am.
That's what Rene Descartes said.
And... sex with strippers?

New Idea for Book:

Butt Cake: An Ode to Human Inquiry.

#25: BEING: THE STINKER

(1)
I poop, thus I am.
I have to eat... to survive.
The poop... is the proof.

BUTT CAKE

What is Butt Cake? It is a mystery. It is an enigma. How can something be so delicious, exciting, and distasteful at the same time? It is a paradox.

I had this thought while sitting on the toilet... and pooping. And, I suddenly became very hungry. And, I was disgusted with myself, because one should not eat, or think about eating, while on the toilet... pooping.

Because... eating is wonderful, and fun (usually). But, pooping is gross, and fowl, or vulgar. Still, eating causes pooping. One generally cannot eat... without later pooping. In essence, doing something wonderful and delicious leads to something gross, fowl, and vulgar. The two actions are opposites. But, they are still connected. Buttcake is a paradox. It is both delicious and disgusting at the same time.

#26: LABOR: FOOD FOR THOUGHT

(1)
Freud says, "Poop is good!"
It, is an accomplishment.
A... Fait Accompli.

#27: SIN: FLUSHING YOUR SINS

(1)
Jesus is the bread.
Satan, and sin, are the poop.
Prayer, flushes it.

BEER CAKE

What is beer cake? Beer cake is... bread. Jesus said "I am the bread of life." This is because he also said, Man can not live on bread alone, but on the Word of God." Jesus is the word of God. Thus, Jesus is the "bread of life."

This is why, for the last supper, during the Jewish Passover (Jesus was Jewish) Jesus gave the "holy sacrament" of "communion", or "holy communion", where we take a blessed wafer or piece of bread, and drink some blessed wine or grape juice (usually in church, or administered by a pastor or priest). Some churches believe that during the sacred rite of communion, the wine and the bread are transformed into the real body and blood of Christ, either during, or after consumption. Other churches believe that it is a holy ceremony that is a metaphor to remember the sacrifice of Jesus Christ to pay for our sins on Earth if we accept his forgiveness.

Jesus said, eat this bread and drink this wine in remembrance of me. This was the night when he was betrayed by Judas, and then crucified and died the next day (Good Friday), which was two days before Easter Sunday (when Jesus rose from the grave and appeared to his disciples (followers), showing that he had conquered death.)

Jason Flick

"The unexamined life is not worth living."
-Socrates
(quote taken from Jones and Wilson, An Incomplete Education)

Jesus said man can not live on bread alone, not because we need meat, fruit, and vegetables... but because man needs spiritual guidance and philosophy to a reason for being, and meaning to life, and to provide a moral guide to living. The philosophy and religion of Christianity provides hope for salvation from the sins of this life... in the afterlife... and heaven.

It has been said that beer is... liquid bread. Beer is fat free and has protein and calories, and can thus provide some nourishment. I am not trying to mess with the sacrament of communion and say that you should substitute beer for wine and communion. But, I am trying to give a tip of the hat to Jesus, and "Make it new." Perhaps one can give thanks to God when drinking a beer, or meet with some friends to talk about the bible and current events.

What exactly is beer? The American Heritage Dictionary of the English Language gives the following adapted definition:

Beer: noun, 1. A fermented alcoholic beverage brewed from malt and flavored by hops. 2. A beverage made from extracts of roots and plants, [West Germanic... probably from Latin bibere, to drink.]
-American Heritage Dictionary, Third Edition, 1992

What is then, beer cake? Beer cake is... bread made from beer. It may not be the best bread, but it's pretty cheap and easy to make. Here's a recipe on how to do it.

DEHYDRATED LIQUID BREAD BREAD (BEER BREAD)

Ingredients:
2 cups flour (general, multi-purpose flour)
1 cup beer (Coors, King Cobra, or Magnum Malt Liquor)
3 tablespoons grated parmesan cheese
1 tablespoon dried parsley
2 tablespoon sugar

Haiku Holiday

2 tablespoon garlic powder
1 and ½ stick of butter or margarine, (12 tablespoons).
1 clean wooden cutting board
1 clean cookie sheet
1 fork
1 tablespoon for measuring
1 sink
1 oven

Directions:

1. Wash hands, be careful not to lose the tablespoon scoop, it is easy to misplace.
   Measure 2 cups of flour and pour into a plastic bowl. Then measure 1 cup of beer and add to the flour in plastic bowl. Stir flour and beer with a fork in a plastic bowl for five minutes. Stir well to mix beer with flour and get air into batter.

2. Cover batter bowl with plastic and put a plate on top. Let sit at room temperature for 30 to 45 minutes.

3. Melt one stick of butter or margarine in a bowl in the microwave for 1 minute.

4. Add 2 tablespoons of parmesan cheese, 1 tablespoon of sugar, 1 tablespoon of parsley,
   1 tablespoon of garlic powder, and stir into the melted butter with a fork.

5. Unwrap batter, pour butter mix into the bread flour batter, and stir with a fork for one minute.

6. Cover batter bowl again and let sit for another 30 minutes at room temperature or warmer.

7. After 30 minutes, uncover the bread batter bowl. Cover a clean wood cutting board, or a cookie sheet (separate from the cookie sheet for baking), with a tablespoon of flour.

8. Pour batter onto flour covered cutting board, or tray. It will be runny and sticky. This is normal. Wash hands as needed.

9. Dust the top of beer bread batter with 2 tablespoons of flour. Then pat lightly and let sit for 3 minutes.

10. Fold dough in half and add another 2 tablespoons (or as needed) of flour. Cover dough with flour, and fold again. Rinse hands to clean off extra sticky dough.

11. Now the dough should get a little more solid. Add another 2 tablespoons of flour and fold in half, and then push dough into a ball.

12. Add another 2 tablespoons of flour, and push the dough ball into a circle. Fold the dough in half. Now is the fun part! Now you get to "knead" the dough; The "Kneading of the dough!"
Pick up the dough and turn it inside out so that the moist sticky dough gets moved to the outside of the dough ball. Squeeze and tear the dough ball with your hands to add air to the dough. You want it to get "stringy."

13. It will now be a sticky ball again. Put dough ball on cutting board. Some dough might stick to your hands. Rinse hands, then add another 2 tablespoons of flour and knead the dough again.

14. Now, take 1 tablespoon sugar, 1 tablespoon garlic powder, and 1 tablespoon parmesan cheese and pour directly onto the dough and knead and push and mix into the dough with hands. Keep pushing, squeezing, and folding.

15. Knead the dough one last time with 2 tablespoons of flour, and fold into a ball with a powdered coat of flour. Place the dough ball into the bowl, and cover and let sit for another ½ hour..

16. Preheat the oven to 400 degrees.

17. Take a clean cookie sheet, and lightly cover it with 1 tablespoon of flour.

18. Uncover the bread dough, and pour onto the kneading surface. Take 1 tablespoon and dust each side of the dough ball with flour.

19. Roll the dough into a "baguette" tube shape bread loaf. Take a fork and poke holes separated by one inch spaces.

20. Place the baguette on a cookie sheet covered with flour, and place in the oven at 400 degrees for 20 minutes.

21. After 20 minutes, take 2 tablespoons of butter or margarine and melt in a cup in the microwave for 30 seconds.

22. Remove the bread from the oven, and drizzle the melted butter over the top with a spoon.
Then, replace the bread in the oven in a different position to avoid burning. Keep the bread in the oven at 400 degrees for another 15 to 20 minutes, and keep an eye on the bottom to make sure it does not get burnt.

23. After 15 to 20 minutes, remove the bread and allow to cool for 10 to 15 minutes. Store in refrigerator. Bone Appetite!

Post Script: Be sure to keep an eye on your tablespoon. I accidentally left mine in the bag of flour, and had to hunt for it... twice! I guess this is a lesson... Don't drink and bake! Or is it don't bake while baked? Or, is it don't bake your drink? Just be sure to make sure you have all the ingredients first, and not to lose your tablespoon, or profanity will become part of the recipe!

Addendum: My buddy Jaime, who is a beer connoisseur, said that a hefeweissen, or a bock beer would be good for this recipe because they have a lot of yeast.

Jason Flick

CAPTAIN'S COURAGEOUS

"As they drove into the confusion, boat banging boat, Harvey's ears tingled at the comments on his rowing. Every dialect from Labrador to Long Island, with Portuguese, Neapolitan, Lingua Franca, French, and Gaelic, with songs and shoutings and new oaths, rattled round him, and he seemed to be the butt of it all. For the first time in his life he felt shy-"

-Rudyard Kipling
Captain's Courageous

One point that I find interesting here, is that the author mentions "Lingua Franca," and then continues to mention, "French," because French IS the Lingua Franca. I would assume that the author is using hyperbole exaggeration to demonstrate the fresh naivete of the young protagonist character here. I find this to be a sweet little detail.

I am attracted to this passage because, having been a Rotary International Exchange Student myself in Brazil as a youth, I know how it feels to be surrounded by foreign language and feel as if everyone is talking about YOU!

This experience, however, taught me about the learning curve of learning a new language, and how there simply is no way to get comfortable with using a new language except to struggle through this initial period of self-doubt and akward self-awareness. I feel that the best way to learn a new language is to "learn by doing," in the tradition of John Dewey.

This would mean making efforts to practice a new language in real-world situations, such as the situation described by Kipling in the previous excerpt... Or, one could visit a local exotic restaurant, like an authentic Mexican restaurant, and practice talking to the waiter or waitress.

However, when in a foreign land, this weakness of ignorance in the local language, can also be turned into an asset, as it provides a window of opportunity to meet new people and make new friends by asking for help with the local, "Lingua Franca," whatever it is.

One should realize, however, that this is not the first character in history to struggle with communicating with strangers in a foreign land. Jesus Christ of Nazareth, himself, was known as the Alpha and Omega, or the Beginning, and the End, in the Greek alphabet. And, although his ministry was focused on Jerusalem, and the holy lands of Israel, he had traveled to and lived in Egypt, and spoke several languages, including Aramaic, Greek, Hebrew, and at least some Latin.

Also, in the bible, a similar scene to the Kipling excerpt is described at the Pentecost. This is when Jesus appeared to a multicultural gathering after his crucifixion, and brought the Holy Spirit to his followers. At this gathering, there were a multitude of strangers and foreigners that spoke many different languages and dialects, but the presence of the Holy Spirit allowed all to speak and understand each other, even though they didn't speak the same language.

Perhaps, something that can be learned from this interesting Kipling excerpt, is that even though the World is a gigantic and strange and mysterious place; a place that is filled with all kinds of exotic lands and cultures and religions, there is still a lot that we share in common as human beings. And, I think that it would be good to remember, that when you encounter someone from one of these strange and distant cultures, to have patience, because you may indeed, one day find yourself... as the mysterious stranger in someone else's home land.

#28: LANGUAGE: LINGUA FRANCA

(1)
One thing I can say,
In almost any language,
Is, "Where's the bathroom?"

(2)
In Spanish I say…
"Donde esta el bano?"
And that does the trick.

(3)
In French, I would say…
"Ou eh toilette, Si vous plaiz?"
That is close enough.

(4)
And, in Portuguese,
"Onde esta, o banho?"
That should do the trick.

(5)
When in Germany?
"Wo ist toilette, bitte?"
You might have to pay!

(6)
And, there's Italian.
Eh, Dove eh Il banio?
There's always… the street!

(7)
Even in England,
It's called a water closet.
Don't hang your clothes there.

(8)
A few foreign words,
Can help make friends all over,
And avoid… mistakes?

Haiku Holiday

#29: FAMILY: VIVA ZAPATA

(1)
Viva Zapata
I like drinking Mexican.
Made in Mexico.

(2)
A one quart bottle;
Corona Familiar,
That means Family Crown.

(3)
32 ounces.
La cerveza mas fina.
It's the most fine beer.

(4)
It's imported beer;
The only gas station glass.
I say glass kicks ass!

(5)
The only beer glass,
That comes in a big bottle;
A double bottle!

(6)
You can re-use it.
You can fill it up with dimes.
Then, buy another.

(7)
Fill it with candy.
Or, fill it with paper clips.
Flowers are nice too.

Jason Flick

(8)
Like a golden crown,
It has brown and tan colors,
Like the beer inside.

(9)
When you pour it out,
It makes a crown of white foam.
It looks like frosting.

(10)
A stream of bubbles;
Float like a sparkling fountain;
Up from the bottom.

(11)
They smell… delicious;
Almost like farts in a tub;
Tastes like… chocolate.

(12)
Corona is great.
It is like rain from heaven…
With chips and salsa.

(13)
Beer is good for you,
When using family jewels…
While on vacation!

(14)
When in Mexico,
Don't drink the water… Drink Beer!
Viva Zapata!

Haiku Holiday

#30: PLEASURE AND PAIN: SMOKING BEER

(1)
Live from Illinois,
It's Saturday Night Splendor;
A beer... and a blunt.

(2)
Imported red star.
Heineken's brewed in Holland.
I'll have a "Heinie"

(3)
It's from Amsterdam.
I hear... they smoke a lot there.
Time, for a cigar!

(4)
Cohiba, sun grown.
The fattest cigar I found.
It's pretty giant.

(5)
Big enough to last,
For a green and silver can,
Of Heine's Lager.

(6)
24 Ounces,
Of premium quality;
Amsterdam's honor.

(7)
I fill the glass mug,
And blow smoke into the glass.
I inhale... and drink.

(8)
It tastes, smooth as silk.
It turns a smoky light brown.
I do it again.

(9)
Now, I blow it slow.
The smoke swirls inside the glass.
The beer... is on FIRE!

(10)
Not really on fire,
But it looks... like it's steaming,
Or, covered in fog.

(11)
It's the only can...
With a green pull tab on top.
They make nice jewelry.

(12)
The glass now empty,
My cigar is half gone.
I think... I might puke.

(13)
I'm okay, I belched.
It was... a false alarm.
No... I'm going to puke.

(14)
Occasional puke,
Is good for your digestion.
Be sure... to have gum.

(15)
Right now, I have gum.
So, I feel clean and refreshed.
Time... for another!

#31: GOOD AND EVIL: VACUUMING VONNEGUT'S VOMIT

(1)
I love vacuuming.
But not if it's for vomit.
Vacuuming is fun.

(2)
It's like mowing grass.
You mow your carpet indoors.
Lots of clean straight lines.

(3)
They have different names.
In Brazil… It's a "Breather."
Um "aspirador."

(4)
Looks like it could mean…
A word for "aspirer."
That's one who aspires.

(5)
And, that's what I was,
When I met Kurt Vonnegut.
I was in high school.

(6)
He came to visit,
A college guest lecturer.
Wrote, "Slaughterhouse Five."

(7)
About fire bombs,
Destroyed Dresden, Germany.
He… was in a film.

(8)
A teen comedy,
That had Rodney Dangerfield.
It's called, "Back to School."

(9)
He included it,
In his biography list.
Everybody loves films.

(10)
He gave three lectures.
At Augustana College,
Marycrest College,

(11)
And St. Ambrose U.
I skipped school all day, that day.
I saw all lectures.

(12)
After one lecture,
It was a small audience.
I got to meet him.

(13)
There were college girls.
They were crowded around him.
"You want to party?:

(14)
"You want to get high?"
I stepped in to ask question.
"Mr. Vonnegut?:

(15)
"I think your book's neat."
"What should I do to write books?"
Then, it got silent.

(16)
Those hot college girls,
They looked so old to me then.
They all looked at me.

(17)
"Read more of my books!"
Kurt Vonnegut said to me.
And, that's what I did.

(18)
Now, the college girls,
They look so young to me, now.
I saw him again...

(19)
Another lecture,
At Galvin Fine Arts Center.
It was a full house.

(20)
He discussed structure.
Georg Wilhelm Friedrich Hegel;
It's pronounced "hey-gal."

(21)
The dialectic structure;
A problem solving method.
Used by Karl Marx too.

(22)
First, there's the "thesis."
The thesis is the problem.
Next, "antithesis."

(23)
It's the opposite,
Or, a proposed solution.
Then, a compromise.

(24)
Or, the end result.
This is called the "synthesis;"
Answer to conflict.

(25)
In literature,
There is a protagonist.
This is the hero...

(26)
The main character.
Then, there's the antagonist.
This is the villain.

(27)
Sometimes... it's a thing.
The story is called a plot.
There is a structure.

(28)
There are three conflicts.
Then the final one... climax.
Then, resolution.

(29)
Then there's an ending.
Each conflict uses Hegel.
Problem, solution...

(30)
Then, an end result.
Thesis, antithesis, then...
The end synthesis.

(31)
Here's demonstration.
Hegel's "beer dialectic."
Take Magnum malt beer.

(32)
It is very strong.
It's a black, gold, white, label.
It's from Miller beer.

(33)
Mix it with a Coors.
Coors Golden Banquet… "classic".
The can looks like bread.

(34)
It's sandy colored.
Thesis and antithesis;
Two different brand beers.

(35)
Mix them together.
A new synthesis flavor…
"Vonnegut's Vomit!"

DAY FOUR: SUNDAY

PEPPY PAUL

WALT WHITMAN

"Flaunt out O sea your separate flags of nations!
Flaunt out visible as ever the various ship-signals!
But do you reserve especially for yourself and for-
the soul of man one flag above all the rest,
A spiritual woven signal for all nation's, emblem-
Of man elate above
Death,
Token of all brave captains and all intrepid sailors-
And mates,
And all that went down doing their duty,
Reminiscent of them, twined from all intrepid-
Captains young or old,
A pennant universal, subtly waving all time,
o'er all brave sailors,
All seas, all ships."

-Walt Whitman
Leaves of Grass, Excerpt from, "Song for All Seas, All Ships."

According to the Blodgett and Bradley Comprehensive Reader's Edition footnotes, this poem was written to commemorate the wreck of the White Star Steamer, Atlantic, that sank of the coast of Nova Scotia in 1873 with a loss of 547 souls. I think it is interesting because it is well known in today's age, because of the popular film, "Titanic", that the White Star company was also the purveyor of the Titanic disaster.

This is just one example, of the powerful historical references that Whitman's works record. Whitman was a dedicated and prolific poet to say the least. Perhaps he was obsessive, maybe even crazy. Yet he even wrote a poem about this, in... "Savantism" Still, with more than 600 poems to his name... he had an insatiable wisdom to share.

It is obvious that he was way way ahead of his time, and he felt an urgency to preserve the themes of his time, for future generations. He wrote poems about... germs... and electricity, at the time of their birth in modern awareness.

The primary fame of his work, I believe, lies in his observations of the American Civil War conflict. Although he looks like... Santa Clause, he serves to tie together the past, his present, and the future. Whitman even has a poem titled, "Medium."

Whitman serves as an observer to bridge the evolution of Colonial America, and the Industrial Revolution. Whitman serves as one of the last crusaders of the "old" world. Whitman was able to achieve such prolific results of more than 600 poems, I imagine, partly because he lived before the time of mass production, electricity, the transcontinental railroad, automobiles, radio, even phonographs, or movies; all that came both with, and from, the industrial revolution.

With the birth of the industrial revolution and the technological advances that it brought, perhaps even language changed? As newspapers, and radios, and television, began to serve as distractions and divertissements for the population, "en masse," so too developed the need for the English Language to grow more abbreviated and proactive. Thus, Whitman represents one of the final frontiers separating the edges... of the romantic, and the scientific. Still, even in his hour of chaos, death, and destruction brought by the American Civil War, Whitman made references to the relevance and significance... and benefits of Christianity. I believe the Christian influence in Whitman's work can be seen in this poem, as well as in others, such as "To Him That Was Crucified," and "Miracles."

Still, I find his most useful and most romantic work, which I had once committed to memory, to be his poem, "To a Common Prostitute." For among the merits that Whitman leaves us, is that if you can read Whitman, it means that you are alive. And... Whitman reminds us, that it's a true blessing to be alive. And, just like in the poem, "Song For All Seas, All Ships," Jesus Christ himself, went down doing his duty, a token of all the brave captains and sailors, a man elate above death, to be a flag... for "all seas, all ships."

#32: HONOR: FULL OF SHIPS

(1)
Is it possible?
Poem, about... a poem?
That is really... weird.

(2)
Well, I'm not Whitman.
For one, I can't grow that beard.
I can still admire.

(3)
Is a poem... gold?
Can the written word... be gold?
The Constitution?

(4)
How much gold was it?
For Democracy's Blueprints?
How many lives lost?

(5)
Freedom is a word.
You can't touch it or see it.
But still, it exists.

(6)
Like ships on the sea,
There's many different freedoms;
Different perceptions.

(7)
There are different types...
There's freedom of enterprise,
There's freedom of choice.

Jason Flick

(8)
There's freedom of time,
I think, the most important…
The freedom of faith.

#33: REVOLUTION: BREAKFAST BEER

(1)
Beer! It's for breakfast!
What? You're kidding. That's crazy.
Is it… so crazy?

(2)
Beer is natural.
It's made from wheat, barley, hops.
Isn't that breakfast?

(3)
They say beer is good,
When you have a hangover…
The hair of the dog?

(4)
Beer with cereal!
Beer and cornflakes with sugar…
Any beer will work.

(5)
A Boston Lager?
Today's beer is Sam Adams.
The Boston Beer Co.

(6)
It's the one pint can.
It's less beer than the others,
But it tastes richer.

Haiku Holiday

(7)
It tastes like coffee.
They must toast the wheat and hops.
It has a rye taste.

(8)
It's Boston Lager.
But, it has a red color.
It looks like acorns.

(9)
A rich sudsy brown,
Maybe it's Boston Water,
That tastes like coffee.

(10)
Dark blue, red, white, gold;
Red, white and blue make the gold,
America's Gold!

(11)
Samuel Adams Beer…
It's an American Name.
He's a patriot!

(12)
He helped fight England;
The war of independence…
A revolution.

(13)
He holds a big mug.
Boston held the tea party.
They wanted more beer.

(14)
The Boston Tea Fest,
1773,
In Boston Harbor.

(15)
Dressed like Indians,
Rebels snuck on British ships.
They tossed the tea out.

(16)
That was a bold move.
It was probably night time;
To protest taxes.

(17)
The British had greed.
So, the patriots fought back...
Against tyranny.

(18)
Sam Adams was IN!
The Continental Congress.
A leader of men.

(19)
From Massachusetts,
He signed the declaration...
To join, or to die?

(20)
Freedom from the Brits!
He became the governor,
In Massachusetts.

(21)
He was against them;
The intolerable acts.
For, red, white, and blue.

(22)
He said, "No Taxes!"...
Without representation.
LIBERTY FOR ALL!

(23)
Independence War!
American Terrorist!
That's Samuel Adams.

(24)
Of course, that was then.
Today, the Brits are our friends.
So, drink beer... and tea!

#34: DEMOCRACY: DEMOCRACY BEER

(1)
Lite Beer from Miller;
They call it fine pilsner beer.
It's a low cal beer.

(2)
Low Calorie's good,
For making a chocolate beer.
It's not chocolate milk.

(3)
One pint, 8 ounces;
That makes 24 ounces...
Of liquid protein.

(4)
It's glowing yellow.
Then, it turns orange and green;
Then, rich chocolate brown.

(5)
Here's how to make it.
Get a pack of M and M's,
Or, use chocolate chips.

(6)
They make a rainbow,
And, they will melt in your beer,
But, not in your hands.

(7)
Drop the M and M's,
Into your cold frothy beer.
Then, watch them dissolve.

(8)
There's candy coating.
Try to pick which color lasts,
And, which color fades first.

(9)
They make a rainbow.
They come in single colors.
They blend in together.

(10)
Chocolate beer is great.
It's just like democracy.
All the colors vote.

(11)
There's red for labor.
There's green for environment.
Blue's Democratic.

(12)
Orange is Libertarian.
Yellow is independent.
Blue's Republican?

(13)
There's Grand Old Party
The Democratic Party.
Agrarian's stopped.

(14)
You get the idea.
All kinds of different options.
Votes are like money.

(15)
You have to have votes,
To get your opinion heard.
Constituency!

(16)
You have to get votes,
To get your voice in congress.
Representation.

(17)
Rainbow of ideas;
Working for compromises.
Finding solutions.

(18)
It's great for dessert.
Chocolate beer is smooth and sweet;
A delicious treat.

MARGARET ATWOOD

"When I get out of here, if I'm ever able to set this down, in any form, even in the form of one voice to another, it will be a reconstruction then too, at yet another remove. It's impossible to say a thing exactly the way it was, because what you say can never be exact, you always have to leave something out, there are too many parts, sides, crosscurrents, nuances; too many gestures, which could mean this or that, too many shapes which can never be fully described, too many flavors, in the air or on the tongue, half-colors, too many."

- Margaret Atwood
The Handmaid's Tale (p.173-174)

#35: PUNISHMENT: JAIL CELL BLUES

(1)
Jail is a bad place.
You should avoid going there.
If you go, take God!

CHRISTIANITY PART I

(1) I have been indoctrinated into, and accepted Christianity as my primary philosophy and religion.

(2) To be a Christian, one accepts certain premises to be reasonable.

(3) The first test, or premise, of Christianity, is of your own existence. I believe and accept that I DO exist, because I experience my tangible senses, I have emotions, I have thoughts, and control of at least some actions of my body.

(4) I accept that I am a human being. I generally share most of the physical traits of other human beings. For example, I walk, and I talk, and I eat, and I sleep, and I have hair (including pubic hair, nose hair?), and hands, and eyes, and feet. The majority of humans have these basic traits. Of course, some humans have suffered accidents, or may have even been born without some of these features. These individuals are of course still human, but are a little different. They may have different talents. A blind person, for example, may have better hearing.

(5) Because I am human, I have human parents. I have a biological mother and father. Or, I have been created from the sperm and egg, or the DNA from other humans.

(6) Where did I come from? How did they create me? Did I exist before I was born? I do not know. I believe that we are created by an invisible and powerful God.

Haiku Holiday

(7) What happens after I die? I believe that I return to the God that created me. My spirit, my being, my personality, my experiences, my feelings, my memory, are what comprise my soul. This soul returns to God in the afterlife. This existence is called, Heaven.

(8) Because God is so grand and powerful that he is our creator, we cannot understand or comprehend him. Because God exists, but is supernatural and beyond our understanding, one must believe and understand God dby faith. Unless, one receives a direct sign or message from God, such as a miracle.

A miracle is an illogical and unexplainable event. This has happened to chosen prophets of God, such as Abraham, Moses, Elijah, and Jesus Christ, and maybe even others. You yourself may have even witnessed or experienced a miracle or a sign, and not known or understood it. God has messengers, such as angels, and the Holy Spirit. God's ways are different than our ways, because we are not God.

(9) How does one have faith or belief in an invisible God? One gains faith by learning what others believe from the Old Testament, and the New Testament of the Holy Bible. The New Testament is the teachings of Jesus Christ, the Son of God. The New Testament was written by others that believe in Jesus Christ as the Son of God, and that knew and witnessed and experienced the miracles from God and angels. This New Testament is proof that other people have experienced and believe the same thing. These people knew and experienced the miracles of Jesus Christ as the Son of God.

(10) How does one experience the supernatural? How does one talk and communicate to God and angels, and experience the presence, knowledge, and miracles of God? If one has faith and believes in an all powerful and creator God, then one can begin to understand and communicate with Jesus Christ, The Holy Spirit, The Angels of God, and God. If one has faith, and belief, then one can begin to experience and understand God and the supernatural and miracles and angels… and Jesus Christ.

(11) Why is Christianity so messy and complicated? Why isn't everyone a Christian? And, why don't all Christians do the same thing? Because, God is not man. God is the creator of man. But God does not want us all to be the same. God created us all differently, and allows us the freedom to be who we are and to make choices and decisions. Even though God created all of us, not everyone will appreciate or understand God in the same way.

(12) What happens while I am alive? Will I do good things or bad things? I do not know. I think that God gives us the freedom to make mistakes. I think that I WILL probably do good AND bad things. But, I think that God wants us to do GOOD things.

GOD'S LIBRARY

How can I believe in a God that I cannot see or touch? Why can't I see or touch God, the creator of Heaven and Earth? We usually do not see or touch God because he is TOO BIG and POWERFUL for us to understand.

Take the sun for example. The Earth revolves around the Sun. We can see the Sun in the sky. We know that it exists. But we cannot touch the Sun, or sunlight. The Sun is so powerful that if we look at it for more than a few seconds, we will burn our eyes and go blind.

We cannot touch sunlight, but we know it exists. Even though we cannot touch sunlight, if we stay too long in the summer sunshine, we will burn our skin. This is called a sunburn. So then, how can we believe, and have faith, and worship, a God that we cannot see or touch?

Here is a metaphor, or an example, of how one can get to know God and have faith that he exists. Consider the idea of a library. In America, most cities have a public library. It is a place where anyone that lives there can go and borrow books to take home for FREE! Many libraries even offer MORE than books. Many libraries offer magazines, DVD movies, computers and internet service to use, music CD's, and phonograph records, that are ALL available to borrow and use ABSOLUTELY FREE!

Some libraries even have equipment that a person can borrow and use such as artwork, fishing poles, video cameras, DVD and VCR players, maybe even tools or scientific equipment to use at home. Again, all of this stuff can be borrowed and used completely free (or nearly free).

And, there is a public library in almost ALL cities! Or, there is a public library in a city nearby. Sometimes, people use the library as a place to have meetings for free. Sometimes, the library will host free music concerts, or movies, or public speakers and lectures. Again, this is usually FREE OF CHARGE! This place sounds too good to be true.

And, the public library is open to everyone that lives in that city. That means that rich people, and poor people, smart people, and uneducated people, beautiful people, and regular people, strong people, and weak people, and people from different countries, or different political parties, or different churches and religions, can ALL use the public library for FREE!

The public library sounds too amazing and too good to be true! It's a place to go and read books, and see movies and concerts for free. It's hard to believe that such a place could exist. BUT, it is true. And, almost every city in America has a public library, or a public library nearby for people to use for free.

BUT, even though public libraries exist, you have to know about it, and find it, and go there, and register, and pick out the books you want, in order to use the library. Even if you do not know about the public library, or if you do not know where it is, or if you do not go there, or if you do not use it; IT STILL EXISTS!

God is the same way. God exists even if you do not know about, or understand him. You have to make the choice to learn about God to discover and experience God yourself. Just like how you have to know about, and go to the library to borrow books for FREE, you have to read the Holy Bible, and the New Testament, and go to church, and go to bible study groups, and go to prayer meetings, get baptized, take holy communion, and most importantly PRAY to Jesus Christ... to get faith in God. Of course, you do not have to do ALL of those things, but those are some ways that you can begin to experience faith in God, and understand God, and talk... to Jesus Christ, the Son of God, in prayer.

Post Script:

I would like to mention, that I have gone to, and I try to go to church to worship. And, I enjoy the benefits of the public library. Previously, I mentioned Sam Adams and "No Taxation Without Representation." I don't know how much the British were taxing the tea. It may have been unreasonable, such as more than 100%. I am not a libertarian. I am not against taxes. Taxes pay for public schools and public libraries. And, if you go to church, donations and fundraisers pay for church. I file my taxes with the government, and I try to donate to church when I attend.

Future Topics:
(1) How do I become a Christian? What do I do?
(2) Who is Jesus Christ?
(3) Why should I become a Christian?

#36: RELIGION: HOLY HAIKU

(1)
Give thanks to the Lord
Pray the Lord's Prayer every day
It's Matthew: Six: Nine

#37: MAN: SUMMER BEER-AID

(1)
From Chippewa Falls,
Where Wisconsin Pride brews smooth,
It's Leinenkugels.

(2)
J. Leinenkugel,
Since 1867.
His name is Jacob.

(3)
Some call it "Leine's"
They make a variety.
It's a classic beer.

(4)
Wisconsin Water,
Is heavy with nutrients.
That's why they make beer.

(5)
This one's for summer.
It has lemons on the can.
It's "Summer Shandy."

(6)
It is a weiss beer,
Brewed like honey lemonade.
It's delicious cold.

(7)
They put art on cans,
From scenic 1950's,
Like Norman Rockwell.

(8)
This can has a lake,
With a cabin and speedboat.
Don't drink and drive boats.

(9)
There's an Indian;
Pretty girl with feather band…
Maybe, half pale face?

(10)
The lemons are big.
They look like they have nipples…
Big juicy nipples!

(11)
If you drink too much,
You might get big juicy nips!
You have to decide.

(12)
It's so delicious.
I could drink it all day long.
Then, I'll have man boobs!

#38: CAUSE: DO THE TO DO

(1)
I make daily lists.
But one day's list… is a week.
I have tons of lists.

(2)
The Persian Gulf War;
General "Norman Schwarzkopf",
Was… "Stormin Norman."

(3)
He gave some advice.
Try to do 3 things a day.
But, his things were… big.

(4)
Here's a couple things,
From some of my to do lists.
Cut my fingernails.

(5)
Women like short nails.
One should be ready to please.
Be sure to brush teeth.

(6)
Keep doctor away.
Eat an apple everyday,
Good for insurance.

(7)
Recycle beer cans.
Do dishes and vacuum floor.
Check the oil in car.

(8)
Get printer cartridge,
And... masturbate every day.
It's good for your health.

(9)
Pay electric bill.
Answer phone calls about car.
Wash load of laundry.

(10)
Check e-mail account.
Be sure to empty trash can.
Buy a revolver.

Jason Flick

THE TO DO LIST

"Why should you read Dante? Jane Austen? Lucretius? Voltaire? Because they are great?
That is no answer. Their greatness is what we feel after we have read them, often years after...

You may rove about virtually at random. The Lifetime Reading Plan is a plan, not a course. You are not required to pass an examination in your knowledge of your children or parents... Plato read at twenty-five is one man, Plato read at forty-five still another... for Hamlet changes into something else as you change into someone else with the passing of the years and the deepening of your sense of life."

This dude, Clifton Fadiman, has a pretty cool book and idea. I think of making a "quest for knowledge," perhaps not unlike that that of Cervantes' famed character, Don Quixote (which is included in Fadiman's list of 100 books.) And, although Fadiman lists 100 great works and authors and provides insight (perhaps like a much more interesting and abbreviated "Cliff Notes", or "Sparks Notes," in my opinion, it is not necessary to feel obligated to read all of these books.

I think that many people today, would be benefited to read just one book from his list of 100 books. I myself, have not yet read any of those books that he mentioned... except for Voltaire (translated). However... there is the danger of reading a bad book. It is hard to "unread" or "unlearn" something that is perhaps dangerous to the human psyche, or "soul".

Jesus Christ said, "What profit's a man, if he gains the world, but loses his soul?" I take this passage to be a cautionary message about the dangers of trying to do too much of anything.
I will paraphrase something Jesus said, which was, "The eyes are the window to the soul, and what you think about is where your heart will be."

In essence, I think that this is a warning, that if you want to be happy, try to think about happy things, and perhaps avoid provocative subjects like... pornography, or... Dante. Personally, as a protestant Christian, I avoid Dante, and Machiavelli, for example.

And, even though I speak Spanish, I have not read Cervantes in the original Castillian (although I know people that have). Mark Twain, who is famed for his many remarks, once commented something like, "One does not have to eat an entire turkey, to know how it tastes."

Still, a literary sojourn to satisfy a thirst for knowledge, can lead one perhaps, to discover magical, and enchanting, and amazing, and even amusing places... in the labyrinth of one's imagination.

I find it ironic, however, that Mr. Clifton Fadiman ends his list of 100 great books... with his OWN book. Still, Fadiman is not the first to promote the virtue of the classics. Fadiman gives a tip of the hat to his predecessors, and mentors, including Mortimer Adler of The Great Books Movement, and author of "How to Read a Book: The Guide to Intelligent Reading." Adler, is renowned as one of the first and most prominent academics to promote the classics as an organized liberal arts curriculum. Fadiman also mentions Mr. William Nichols, editor of This Week magazine, as a predecessor, and includes Mr. Charles Van Doren as his collaborator.

I imagine that it is true, what they say, that "Knowledge is Power." And, how, and what, and when and where you choose to read the classics is up to you. But, in reflection of the eternal, I believe that it is also important to take time... to live life and enjoy our time in the present.

#39: TIME: THE HOURGLASS

(1)
Time is the essence,
Of the life we live on Earth.
It keeps moving on.

(2)
There's no way to change,
What has already happened.
That's most of the time.

(3)
So, it's important,
To be grateful for blessings:
Love, family, friends.

(4)
Easy to forget,
The things that are important...
Making memories.

(5)
On the other hand,
The future gives us something...
For hopes, dreams, and plans.

(6)
When I read a book,
I can touch the eternal.
I lose track of time.

(7)
Jesus prayed daily,
Not afraid to be alone;
Not afraid... of time.

(8)
I try to save time,
By using a microwave.
It cooks really fast!

(9)
Still, I'm always late.
And, it makes people angry.
Always... tomorrow!

#40: IMAGINATION: DONUT HOLE

(1)
G. Heileman Co.,
Brewed since 1851,
Presents you… "Stag Beer!"

(2)
Stag beer is special.
It's the cheapest beer I found;
Economical.

(3)
In a half quart can,
It costs less than a dollar.
That's for one whole pint!

(4)
It's less than a buck,
But, there's a buck on the can;
A buck… for a buck!

(5)
I see three faces.
The left profile of a deer;
That's why it's called "Stag."

(6)
There's another face.
The deer's chin… looks like a smile!
With 2 eyes and nose.

(7)
The nose is a dot;
To the left of the left eye.
Then, two eyes above.

(8)
The left deer eye's one.
To the right is the other.
It looks… like a clown.

(9)
There is a third face.
It looks… like a bear, or dog;
Looking up and right.

(10)
Right eye, above nose.
The nose, is the ear of bear;
Looking… at antler.

(11)
Below deer's left eye,
There's a curve, that makes the mouth.
The left eye's… a nose!

(12)
You need the donuts!
I'm drinking beer and donuts;
Tastes like apple pie!

(13)
I bought day old glazed.
Cut one into eight pieces.
Then, dunk them… with fork.

(14)
Another secret!;
The can looks just like the beer.
It's a can of GOLD!

(15)
I forgot something.
It's about eating donuts!
And, it's important!

Haiku Holiday

(16)
Take the leftovers,
And… slide them on your penis!
THEN… feed your girlfriend(s).

(17)
Ladies… can do it!
Take one, and put between legs…
Insert tongue, enjoy!

(18)
It's not that healthy…
But, verrrry satisfying.
That's… beer and donuts!

DAY FIVE: MONDAY

GEORGE ON BREAK

SUP SALINGER?

"After the movie was over, I started walking down to the Wicker Bar, where I was supposed to meet old Carl Luce, and while I walked I sort of thought about war and all. Those war movies always do that to me. I don't think I could stand it if I had to go to war. I really couldn't...

My brother D.B. was in the army for four god dam years. He was in the war, too. He landed on D-Day and all- but I really think he hated the army worse than the war. I was practically a child at the time... He didn't have to shoot anybody. All he had to do was drive some cowboy general around all day in a command car. He once told Allie and I that if he'd had to shoot anybody, he wouldn't have known which direction to shoot in. He said the Army was practically as full of bastards as the Nazis were.

I remember Allie once asked him wasn't it sort of good that he was in the war because he was a writer, and it gave him a lot to write about and all... I'm sort of glad they've got the atomic bomb invented. If there's ever another war, I'm going to sit right the hell on top of it."
-J.D. Salinger, The Catcher in the Rye (p.181-183)

One of the things that I love about The Catcher in the Rye, are the contemporary references for that time. I was blessed with the opportunity to work for a global transportation company in New Jersey for several years. I lived in Hoboken, NJ, which is the home of baseball, and Frank Sinatra. Hoboken is the square mile city, but with recent urban renewal, people call it the "sixth burrow" of NYC because it's only 10 minutes by train or ferry. New York City is the greatest city in the World! It really is... "The city that never sleeps."

Sometimes, I would work a night shift, and then go out at 3:00 a.m. I would love to visit the all night bodegas with their diverse snacks... genoa salami sandwiches from Little Italy, fresh authentic NYC bagels, cold NYC pizza, single bottles of beer. Then I would smell the flowers. Maybe someday I'll write a book about a New York City bodega... Food, Flowers, and Fags! A fag is a double meaning. In America, a fag is a gay. In England, a fag is a cigarette. The bodegas sell smokes. Of course, I am probably romanticizing those days. It was probably a lot dirtier, darker, crowded, competitive, lonely, and I was probably a lot more broke than I remember. Still, I would love to go back, and try and find, "The Wicker Bar."

The Catcher in the Rye is one of those books that appeal to all ages. As a teenager, I first got turned on to "The Catcher in The Rye" because of the profanity and graphic language, and the fantasy of youthful independence. Later in life, however, the story reveals many layers of a darker nature and the struggle of learning to be a part of the world at large (growing pains), and learning to become comfortable with oneself. In this tradition of self discovery, I believe it was Socrates, that stated the merit of getting to "know thyself." However, in this excerpt, one can witness one of the other great aspects of "The Catcher", which is the historical references to the post WWII growing pains of modern society. J.D. Salinger really struggled to push the envelope and reveal his truths that he perceived and observed about modern society. In a sense, perhaps Salinger bared his soul to serve as… "The Catcher in the Rye." It must not have been easy for a native New Yorker to express compassion for the Nazis in post WWII society, as Salinger does with such casual finesse in this passage.

Salinger advocates a war against the "phonies", and I can recall a similar battle in the New Testament when Jesus Christ proclaims us to all be hippocrites… and "phonies." Jesus suggests that we should all pull the plank out of our own eye before pulling the speck out of our neighbors eye. Or, in other words- we should judge not, lest we be judged (we should not judge other people without walking a mile in their shoes). As Salinger was himself, a WWII veteran, and wrote other stories about veterans and WWII- I think that the brother character… D.B.…. is him, Salinger himself.

#41: TYRANNY: SALINGER SOUP

(1)
Teddy Roosevelt
Said… walk soft, but with a stick.
This is what I think.

(2)
War is terrible.
Someone once said "War is Hell!"
Sometimes, it must be.

(3)
U.S. is prepared.
M.A.D. deters big wars.
During, The Cold War.

(4)
M.A.D. warns us,
Mutually Assured Death!
Everybody dies!

(5)
War can give freedom!
The fall of the Berlin Wall,
Was a victory.

(6)
Ending tyranny,
From Eastern Communism,
And its oppression.

(7)
But, diplomacy…
Should be the first line defense.
Because… war is hell.

(8)
There are other wars,
That are always being fought.
Such as business wars.

(9)
Wars between school teams,
Remind us that fights, exist.
One must stay alert.

(10)
Conflicts will exist.
That's just the way of the world.
But, we can prepare.

(11)
When people behave,
We can avoid violence.
And, try to stop war.

(12)
I just lost a friend,
Who was a World War II Vet.
They suffered a lot.

(13)
They did not have help,
For... post traumatic stress stuff.
He spent time... alone.

(14)
The Vietnam Vets...
Still suffer from these problems.
It's still a problem.

(15)
The Dessert Storm Op.,
Defeated a tyranny.
Wars will come to pass.

Haiku Holiday

(16)
Ike Eisenhower;
Military Industry…
He said, to beware.

(17)
Jesus talked of war.
He said, they will come to pass.
We must… pray for peace.

#42: WORLD: FISH N CHIPS ALE

(1)
You can smoke in bars.
That's one good reason to go.
And, chicks have big boobs!

(2)
World's best fish and chips.
I'm talking about England.
Home of the Union Jack.

(3)
Union Jack's the flag;
Same colors as the U.S…
That's kind of spooky.

(4)
Still, chicks have big boobs!
It's… because of fish and chips.
Fish and Chips for Boobs!

(5)
You don't have to go.
Drink Olde English Malt Liquor…
Eat, fish sticks and fries!

(6)
England's got bad news...
The bars close at 10 p.m.
That stops soccer fights.

(7)
Soccer fights are bad.
England calls soccer... football.
They still play rugby.

(8)
No U.S. Football!
Rugby's... like, U.S. Football;
But... without the rules.

(9)
In England... drink fast!
In U.S., drink... Olde English!
It's called, "800".

(10)
Is... that calories?
Don't know what 800 is...
But, it tastes real smooooth.

(11)
24 ounces.
It's the Olde English Brew Co.
It's from... Milwaukeeeee!

(12)
One pint, 8 ounces.
In a Royal can... with crowns;
Burgundy and gold.

(13)
Enough about beer;
In England, French fries are... chips!
That's... fish and French fries.

Haiku Holiday

(14)
Fish sticks and French fries,
Make a great meal together,
With... Olde English Ale.

(15)
Cook them separately.
I add butter and garlic.
It's not... deit food!

(16)
Some use tartar sauce,
As... a condiment... for fish.
I... eat my fish, plain.

(17)
Did you get the joke?
Fish, HERE, is... a vagina!
Same... in ALL countries.

(18)
I add other stuff;
Parmesan, parsley, pepper...
For a gourmet meal.

(19)
Some use... vinegar?
I eat my French fries with sauce.
I eat my fish plain.

(20)
Now, I am talking,
Really, about eating food.
Still... sauces are fun!

(21)
French fries deserve more.
I use... EVERY sauce I can.
I pour them in cups.

(22)
Why are they... FRENCH fries?
They should be American!
BELGIUM... has the best.

(23)
Ketchup is classic.
Mustard is calorie free.
Don't forget... mayo!

(24)
There's barbeque sauce,
There's thousand island dressing,
And, ranch is good too!

(25)
There's spicy mustard.
Honey... is my favorite.
Just don't forget... BEER!

CERTAINLY CERVANTES

"As to your worship's valour, courtesy, and exploits," continued Sancho, "there are different opinions. Some call you mad but droll: others, valiant but unfortunate; others, courteous but impertinent. Then they go sticking their noses into so many things that they don't leave a whole bone wither in you worship or in myself."

"Remember, Sancho, "said Don Quixote, "that whenever virtue is found in an eminent degree it is persecuted. Few or none of the famous men that have lived escaped being slandered by malicious tongues... Alexander, whose deeds of prowess earned him the name of Great, was held to be somewhat of a drunkard."
-Cervantes, Don Quixote (p. 245)

Karl Marx, Socrates, Plato, Aristotle, Moses, Allah, Buddha, and even the Beatles have had to suffer or endure ridicule, humiliation, and disapproval, for making a stand for their ideas. John Lennon of the Beatles, made a protest for Peace during the Vietnam War, by staging an international interview from a hotel bed with his wife in Amsterdam, and it later became the object of one of his songs.

> "Christ you know it ain't easy. You know how hard it can be.
> The way things are going, They're going to crucify me."
> -John Lennon

I am not a martyr. I am not Jesus Christ. I am not God. I am not a prophet. I am not a megalomaniac. I am not even a preacher. I am… a Christian.

I worship Jesus Christ as the son of God, who was born from the Virgin Mary, conceived by the Holy Spirit, related to King David of the Jews, baptized by John the baptist, and predicted by the prophets Isaiah, and Elijah, and in the book of Psalms. He made miracles, healed the sick, and ministered the good news of the New Testament.

He suffered under Pontius Pilate (The Roman Governor), was crucified on the cross in Jerusalem, as an innocent man. His death served as a sacrifice to pay for the sins, and provide forgiveness before God, of all people that accept him as their savior, and accept his forgiveness. Two days after his burial, he was resurrected, and rose from the grave to prove that he is the son of God, and that he had conquered death, and that his promise of forgiveness of sins, and eternal life with God, is real, and true.

Jesus is called "The Great I Am", by some, both because he had faith in God, and stood up for what he believed in, and lived as a leader and a mentor, or example for loving each other.
But, also, because it says in The Holy Bible, that in the beginning of time, God was the word, and the word was God, and God spoke, and made the word real. And, Jesus said, "I Am," and he became real. This is important because it shows how The Bible IS the word of God, and Jesus made the word of God REAL by reading it, teaching it, preaching it, living it, doing it… and fulfilling prophecy to make it come true.

Even though, when he was alive he suffered humiliation, ridicule, mockery, was persecuted, and tortured because of his ministry and beliefs, he stayed strong and firm in his faith, beliefs, and philosophy. His philosophy came down to two rules: (1)Love God, and (2) Love your neighbor (fellow human beings).

#43: VIRTUE AND VICE: CERVANTES CERVEZA

(1)
Virtue is noble.
Virtue is doing what's true.
Virtue's dignified.

(2)
Virtue is honest.
Virtue is doing the right thing.
It's honorable.

(3)
Vice is opposite.
Vice is doing sinful things.
Vice is temptation.

(4)
Vices are weakness.
Illicit sex is a vice.
That's prostitution.

(5)
Gambling is a vice.
Guards gambled while Jesus died.
It's in the Bible.

(6)
Drugs can be a vice.
Recreational drug use.
Using narcotics.

Haiku Holiday

(7)
Vice is nice, sometimes.
Too much virtue is a vice.
Man's good, AND evil.

(8)
Manichean thought;
The duality of man.
We are strong, AND weak.

(9)
But, we have free will.
Moderation is the key.
We can work… AND play.

(10)
Don Quixote fought,
Against the dragons of vice.
Cervantes, from Spain.

(11)
Brewed in Mexico,
Modelo Especial.
It's Mexican Beer.

(12)
White, Blue, Silver, Gold;
Modelo Cerveza's grand!
Elegant import.

(13)
It's delicious beer.
Lower cost of production,
High quality taste.

(14)
It's a good dessert.
With a full rich creamy taste.
Just a little… lasts.

(15)
We're virtue and vice.
Just like salsa and good beer.
Moderation's good.

(16)
Salsa is virtue.
But, beer can become a vice.
We're salsa and beer.

EMERGENCY SALSA

Here's a recipe for if you need some salsa in an emergency, but don't have any. You can make... home made salsa. Here's a quick and easy recipe.

Ingredients:
1. ½ cup ketchup
2. 1 tablespoon garlic powder
3. 1 tablespoon onion powder
4. 2 tablespoons parsley
5. 1 tablespoon cilantro or coriander or chives
6. 1 teaspoon chili powder
7. 1 teaspoon pepper
8. 1 teaspoon paprika
9. 12 tablespoons beer
10. 2 onions
11. 1 bag of tortilla chips, or crackers.

Directions:
1. Pour ½ cup ketchup into mixing bowl, or jar.
2. Pour six tablespoons of beer into separate cup.
3. Add 1 tablespoon garlic powder to beer and stir.
4. Add 1 tablespoon onion powder to beer and stir.
5. Add 2 tablespoons parsley to beer and stir.
6. Add 1 tablespoon cilantro or coriander or chives to beer and stir
4. Add 1 teaspoon chili powder to beer and stir.
5. Add 1 teaspoon of pepper to beer and stir.

6. Add 1 teaspoon of paprika to beer and stir.
7. Add mixed beer to ketchup and stir (or close lid and shake if in jar)
8. Take 2 onions and cut off top and bottom ends of onions.
9. Rinse onions.
10. Peel off skin and outer layer of onion.
11. Cut onions in half vertically from top to bottom.
12. Cut onions into ¼ inch slices horizontally (sideways)
13. Chop these slices into ¼ inch pieces
14. Add onion to ketchup and stir (or close lid and shake if in jar)
15. Add 6 more tablespoons of beer and stir or shake.
16. Optional ingredients to add are 1 tablespoon sugar, 1 chopped tomato, 1 chopped jalapeno
17. Shake and stir salsa, and let sit and marinate for a few minutes.
18. Do not freeze. This salsa will keep in the refrigerator for 1 week.
19. serve with chips or crackers and cold beer.

HYPNOTIC QUIXOTIC

This is a poem that is not a haiku. I'm including it, because it is relevant to Cervantes.
If you don't know already, Cervantes famed work, Don Quixote is about chivalry and the romantic idealist nobleman, Don Quixote, that would attack windmills thinking they were dragons.

Interestingly, although many relate windmills to Holland, there are many windmills in Spain. Cervantes and Don Quixote are very popular in Spain, and Mexico. I spent a summer as an English teacher in the beautiful and romantic city of Guanajuato, Mexico. Guanajuato is one of the world's richest silver mines. Before Mexico hosted a revolution for its independence from Spain, it was a Spanish colony, just like America was a colony of Britain.

While Mexico was under Spanish control, they built the silver mines, and castles and fortresses to protect the silver in Guanajuato. These castles and fortresses still stand, and Guanajuato has a medieval European feel to this day. They have cobblestone roads, and plazas with fountains. Visiting Guanajuato is like taking a trip in time.

Jason Flick

As Guanajuato had strong ties to Spanish royalty, they chose Cervantes and Don Quixote as their town mascot. As a university town, and the state capitol, Guanajuato has a thriving art scene. Guanajuato is the birthplace of Diego Rivera. Cervantes holds strong as a town theme, however, as they host an annual world renowned festival called the Cervantina Festival, that has been frequented by the Spanish Royal Family.

Spain had a hand in the United States as well. Dubuque, Iowa is home to the Spanish Lead Mines from when it was a Spanish Territory. There is still a park there to preserve the historical mines. Ironically, Cervantes and Spain have a modern day influence on America as well, as America is currently undergoing a "renewable energy revolution." Windmills are currently popping up all over the country. There are two giant 12 story windmills less than a mile from my house. Many of these modern windmills come from Spain. Thus, even today…
Don Quixote lives!

HYPNOTIC QUIXOTIC

Windmill why do you keep me up all night?
You keep spinning round til the morning light.
The wind keeps blowing, but there's no where to go.
Why do you keep spinning? I just don't know.

Windmill why do you keep me up all night?
You keep spinning round til the morning light.
The wind keeps blowing, there's no need to fight.
But, still, you keep on spinning, whether it's day or night.

But, sometimes I can see your point.
Life goes on, even when you disappoint.
Sometimes there are things I wish I didn't know.
But, since you keep spinning round, why don't you give us a show?

You stand so strong, but you wear your heart on your sleeve.
I guess, you think there's no need to deceive.
You keep spinning fast like you're going out of style.
But, if you're going to last, you need to relax once in a while.

Haiku Holiday

Postscript:

This is not part of the poem. Here are a few comments about the "RENEWABLE ENERGY REVOLUTION". I live near some windmills, and they do NOT keep me up at night as the poem suggests. That comment is simply a tool used for dramatic effect. I find the windmills to be aesthetically appealing when they are on the flatlands. I use these local windmills as a landmark to help me find my way home off the highway and keep from missing my exit.

RENEWABLE ENERGY REVOLUTION

I think that renewable energy is in America's best interest, and in the best interest for the environment and future generations. God bless America, and thank God for our highways and automobiles and an abundance of petroleum products. I am not against the Rockefeller's, and Standard Oil, and Oil companies. Standard Oil, and Henry Ford helped build America's infrastructure, and build a middle class. The post WWII Eisenhower highway system helped expand economic opportunities and tourism. I have driven on the historic route 66 from Chicago to Los Angeles, and I highly recommend it.

However, it is no secret that there are alternative energy sources available. I have witnessed cars that run on alcohol made from sugar cane when I lived in Brazil. It is also no secret that gasoline cars cause pollution that is harmful to the environment, and create "smog".
There are cars that use solar energy, and electric batteries, and natural gas. It has been hypothesized that cars could be built to run on salt water. Now, the auto industry is finally investing in alternative energy and hybrid cars. There are also many other forms of alternative and renewable energy for energy needs. There is wind energy, clean coal, natural gas, solar enegy, hydroelectric energy, and some have argued for corn alcohol, and even oil created from algae.

These alternative energy sources, such as wind energy, help create new economic opportunities and careers. I think that it is also beneficial for America to reduce its dependence on imported petroleum. As America is a relatively free market economy, those with resources in the petroleum industry, should join this revolution, and allocate some assets towards harvesting these alternative energy sources. This can be a win-win opportunity for investors.

#44: PROGRESS: RENEWABLE ENERGY REVOLUTION

(1)
There's so much to say,
About new technology.
It's always changing.

(2)
The Pony Express,
Was replaced by telegraph,
Then, the telephone.

(3)
Progress involves change.
Progress means to improve it.
Not, to stay the same.

(4)
The new gold rush is…
Alternative energy.
It's for the future.

(5)
Big oil companies,
It's time to pull your own weight.
Invest in future.

(6)
Petroleum was…
The start of our industry.
Built… America.

(7)
But it's time for change.
Get ready for tomorrow.
Invest in future.

(8)
Apples and Oranges;
From fossil fuel, or the wind,
We need energy.

(9)
For America,
It helps us save resources,
And make dollars last.

(10)
And, for the whole world;
Leads the way for tomorrow;
Helps to save the Earth.

(11)
Renewable E,
Helps man live in harmony;
Helps democracy.

(12)
It's not just a dream.
Some American cities,
Have free internet.

(13)
One last thing I'll say.
If I was king for a day,
FREE energy day!

Post script: This renewable energy revolution and free energy idea follows Cervantes and Don Quixote, because it is somewhat idealistic, and yet, possible. Also, I would like to see...
free cocaine?

INGENIUS U.

YOU can be an INGENIOUS! Not everyone can be a genius. Who are some famed geniuses? There's Einstein, Alexander Graham Bell, Thomas Edison, Henry Ford, Tesla, Da Vinci, Marconi, Oppenheimer, Michelangelo, Bill Gates and Steve Jobs (These names are picked and listed at random for meritorious achievements, I do not know if they were actually "geniuses.") Technically, I think a genius is someone that has a very high I.Q (Intelligence Quotient), from an I.Q. test, and I don't think I.Q. tests were invented until the 1940's, or 1950's.
So, there's no way to know for sure if Leonardo Da Vinci was a certified "genius."

It is pretty rare to be a genius. However, we can all be an "ingenius." An ingenius is one that practices ingenuity, or problem solving skills. An "ingenius" is a problem solver. Some famous ingeniuses might be Joseph Stalin, or Ghenghis Khan. They solved problems (usually by killing people). I jest, however, as they may have been psychopaths too. An ingenius does not need to be a psychopath. Some other famous ingeniuses might be Paul Revere, or Orville and Wilber Wright (inventors of the airplane). An ingenius could be a nice bank teller that does you a favor, and finds a way to sign you up for overdraft protection that covers your checking account for negative balances... after you have already bounced a check. Perhaps Marilyn Monroe could be considered an "ingenius" by making people feel good by giving them a smile and a wink.

It has been said that Americans are "practical," and that Americans are problem solvers.
It has been said that Americans have a "can do" attitude and spirit. Americans are... ingenuitive.
Americans are... "ingeniuses." Americans idealize efficiency. Americans have a history of finding a way to "get it done," whatever it takes.

Some people have suggested that the success of America is due to two things: (A) American Democracy and its constitutional freedoms, and (B) "The Pioneer Spirit." This pioneer spirit has its roots from America being a "New World," and a new experiment in democracy that offered new beginnings and opportunities for a variety of diverse cultures. Because many of Americans came from somewhere else, they were excited and enthusiastic to seek new opportunities, try new things, and solve problems to do what it takes to "get it done."

The practical nature of the American "Pioneer Spirit" has been discussed in Alexis de Tocqueville's, *Democracy in America*, and, Frederick Law Olmsted's. *"The Closing of The American Frontier."*

#45: CONSTITUTION: FUCK OFF... PLEASE

(1)
The Constitution,
A guarantee of freedom,
Grants freedom of speech.

(2)
You cannot slander,
And spread lies about people.
You CAN say... Fuck Off!

(3)
There's Australian Beer.
It's known as Foster's Lager.
It's a HUGE blue can.

(4)
Red, White, Blue, and Gold.
Here in the states, it's Texan.
In Texas... all's BIG.

(5)
From Fort Worth Texas;
Original recipe...
Melbourne, Australia.

(6)
Here in the U.S.;
25 point 4 ounces.
And, it's union made.

(7)
Australia's real far;
The other side of the world...
Southern Hemisphere!

(8)
They say, when you flush,
Water spins counter-clockwise.
They're counter-culture.

(9)
Originally,
Australia was run by Brits.
It was a prison.

(10)
Britain sent convicts,
To the farthest place they could.
That's what I have heard.

(11)
One can imagine,
"Twas" likely short time before,
They stated, "Fuck Off!"

(12)
They're pioneers too.
A New World... with lots of space,
Run by Great Britain.

(13)
Still, they're not like us.
They're like... America Lite.
They're part of Britain.

(14)
A Democracy,
But, voting is required.
It's optional here.

(15)
They speak English... but,
We have football, and baseball.
They're rugby, cricket.

(16)
It's just as big though,
If you don't count Alaska.
They have... Foster's Beer.

(17)
I like Foster's Beer.
To me, it tastes like blue cheese.
Maybe, that's just me.

(18)
There's a Kangaroo,
Southern Cross Constellation,
The letters... F. O.

(19)
Freedom of Speech Rocks!
It's in the Constitution.
Love you, but... Fuck Off!

PROGRESS AND EVOLUTION

Right now, just now at this exact moment, it started raining outside. Not just raining, but pouring. It is pouring and thundering, so I have to stay in and get some things done. I need to work on my personal internet website to promote my other book, The Intermission: Solitaire, Beer, and Heaven. I love playing solitaire. Especially on the computer.

It is a spring storm. It is the fun kind, tropical, hot, and wet (just like my fantasy lover).
I am watching a syndicated television re-run of a popular program called, "The Office." It is a show about life working in... an office.

Jason Flick

I should write a t.v. show and call it, "Unemployed." It could be the opposite of, "The Office."

I am watching television on a new "digital" t.v. If you recall, in my book the Inter-Mission, I discussed briefly the transfer into the digital age; The Dawn of The Digital Age.
The true opening and launch of the digital age could be traced back to several events.

According to the 2005 World Almanac, There was the birth of IBM in 1924. the ENIAC computer in 1946, (which took up a whole room) the transistor in 1947, the integrated circuit in 1958, finally, the microprocessor in 1971. The microprocessor led to the creation of practical and usable office computers. In 1975, Microsoft was founded by Bill Gates and Paul Allen. In 1976, Apple Computer was founded by Steve Jobs and Steve Wozniak, who gave us The Apple II, the first popular home computer. In 1981, IBM introduced the PC, or Personal Computer with the Microsoft DOS operating system. In 1984, Apple came out with the Macintosh, the first computer with a mouse. In 1990, Microsoft introduced Windows 3.0 for home and office use.
In 1991, LINUX was invented by Swedish student, Linus Torvalds and made free for public use on PC computers. By 2002, one billion computers had been manufactured in total.

After the microprocessor was invented, the internet was expanded, and later the cell phone was created. I still remember my first cell phone and ATM card in 1998. I used a prepaid card that cost a dollar a minute. In 1969, the ARPNET was created by the U.S. government. In 1988 the public usable internet was created by Finnish student Jarkko Oikarinen with IRC (Internet Relay Chat). Then in 1989, the world was really changed, when Tim Berners Lee invented the World Wide Web (www). Or, perhaps the internet really changed the world with the invention of the browser, from Mark Andreesen's Mosaic, which helped lead to Netscape in 1994.

What was the true opening and launch of the digital age then? What was it that opened the "digital frontier?" Was it the birth of I.B.M., and the ENIAC computer? Was it the birth of the personal computer? Was it the birth of the "Ying-Yang" Manichean conflict between

I.B.M.'s PC and Microsoft, and Bill Gate's Windows, versus Steve Jobs and Apple Computers?
Or, was it the birth and growth of the internet revolution, with the creation of Marc Andreesen's Mosaic, Netscape, America Online, and search engines like Yahoo, Google, Ask Jeeves, and Bing? Or, was it the inception of personal websites like Napster, Friendster, MySpace, Facebook, and Twitter, and Second Life?

Perhaps the Dawn of the Digital Age began with the switch from VHS and VCR's to DVD's, and from vinyl L.P. records and 8 track tapes, and audio cassette tapes, to compact disc cd's? I say... NAY. The true naissance of the digital age... was June 11th, 2009, when American Television made the official switch from analog to digital television. This was one of the most interesting changes I have witnessed in my lifetime. When television screens all across America went from flourescent pixeled glass screens of fluid blurred color... to grey white noise, and then to black empty space. Only to re-ignite again, in an explosion of digital and high definition "electric fireworks."

The only problem? Reception. As I sit in my rural location during a thunderstorm, I can feel the effects of digital reception. Many feel, the effects of the digital dial, as the t.v. reception is... questionable. When it works... it is nothing short of "fabulosity!" But, as many will be quick to tell you, it doesn't always work. Digital television seems to be... an all or nothing venture. Digital television is "super duper" those that manage to get good reception, or can afford cable. And, digital televisions are more portable, compact, lighter (mostly plastic), and even cheaper, than the old glass screen dinosaurs.

At the time of the digital television switch, the government offered free coupons to buy a digital converter box, so that you could switch your old analog T.V. to the new digital reception.
That's what I have. I wish that I would have bought a bunch of them. After the digital switch, people were giving away their old t.v.'s, even throwing them away in the garbage!

That's where I got my t.v.... the garbage! I now have a collection of three t.v.'s that I got for free. If I would have bought a bunch of those digital converters, I could have had a hundred t.v.'s! My "free" t.v. is fine. A nice big Sony "Trinitron." But, it weights as much as five, or maybe even ten, digital t.v.'s. I'm hoping that one day... It will be worth a lot of money as a collector's item; my "antique" television.

Digital television, then, is perhaps anti-democratic for those left behind without the lifeblood of the "American Grand Illusion"... which is T.V. Those that can't afford, or get reception, or afford cable T.V. got cut off from popular culture. Rural couch potatoes, for example, are left behind... in digital darkness. It is as if they were whisked back in time to the other... dark ages. Of course, for such rural saps (like myself), there are still cell phones, dvd players, notebook computers (with cellphone wireless broadband plug-in modems that provide 24 hour wireless access internet from anywhere you go (I have one, they're new to the market).

Technically, they even make cell phones with built in internet mini-tv's. Lastly, there is always there is always the digital "counter-culture"; the "underground railroad" of digital media; the last line of defense in the digital media conglomerate network. This last line of defense allows, even the Native Americans living on a reservation in the Grand Canyon to access the digital television framework; perhaps the salvation of our nation... Digital Satellite Network Television.

Post Script: Currently, there are two major satellite dish network companies. There is "Dish Network," and "Direct T.V."

#46: EVOLUTION: SMART PHONE PHONY

(1)
I remember it;
My first wireless cell phone;
1998.

(2)
For emergencies,
It was for phone calls only.
It was a pre-pay.

Haiku Holiday

(3)
I had to buy it.
It was a buck a minute.
There was no contract.

(4)
All it did was call.
Now, they have tv on phone!
They call it "smart phone."

(5)
The new phones are hard.
You can use the internet.
Or, listen to songs.

(6)
You read a book.
You can play video games.
You can watch movies.

(7)
The screen is still small.
Still, it's like my wildest dreams.
It fits in pocket.

(8)
It's got calendar.
It can show you the weather.
You can ask questions!

(9)
Where's a gas station?
You can take pictures with it.
And, make movies too.

(10)
The smart phone is like…
Digital swiss army knife.
It can do a lot.

(11)
You can write letters.
You can record messages.
Make video calls!

(12)
You can see people,
While talking to them on phone.
You can moon them too.

(13)
You can take pictures,
And, put them on internet.
Take pics of your "junk"!

(14)
Now, I only pay,
Fifty dollars a month for...
Unlimited calls!

(14)
They have maps on phone.
I have maps... of the whole world!
But there's one problem.

(15)
With all of that stuff,
It's hard to make a phone call,
If... battery's dead.

PASSWORD PISSED

Cock sucking shit fuck faggot bitch! Rat hole piss fucker hoe bitch mutherfuckin crumb bum piece of shit son of a bitch! Passwords! We got so many of dem dese days- It finally finally motherfuckin happened. I finally fuckin forgot one of my passwords. Son of a bitch! Now I gotta try tah figger it out. Too many passwerds. We gotta have a friggin passwerd fer da ATM ting, a passwerd fer da computer, a passwerd fer da phone. In dis case, I wanna use my friggin computer, and I friggin fergot da passwerd. So, not only can I NOT do my friggin werk, but I can't use dat computer til I figger it out.

Possible passwords? Well I didn't want tah write em down because I may need tah use em. So dat means I gotta try tah remember and write down all da passwerds I mighta tried tah use.

#47: EXPERIENCE: PASSWORD POOP

(1)
Computers are here.
Everything uses passwords.
They're all connected.

(2)
We need protection.
To protect identity,
And for privacy.

(3)
Passwords protect us.
They protect us from all theft.
But, they're annoying.

(4)
I have three passwords;
Low level, medium, high.
This keeps it simple.

(5)
Low is general.
This is for advertisements.
Like, contest pages.

(6)
Medium is there,
For middle important things,
Like insurance forms.

(7)
High is top secret.
This is for private email,
Or, for bank account.

(8)
Some write things backwards.
Some use birthdays of close friends.
Just don't use… "Password."

(9)
Safeword's something else.
Don't use password for safe word…
You'll get stiff at work!

GOD AND SCIENCE, FAITH AND REASON

Jesus and the "self-fulfilling prophecy?" A self-fulfilling prophecy can be a good thing, or a bad thing. A self-fulfilling prophecy is when you think about something a lot, and then it comes true. This can be used as an educational tool in a positive way. For example, if you are a piano player, and you want to be an award winning concert pianist, then you think about it a lot, and you do things to make it come true. You practice the piano. You take lessons. You study music and music history. You go to watch other pianists in concert. You investigate what they did to be a success. You ask for advice. Then, you think about it, and dream about it, and try to make it real. This is a positive self-fulfilling prophecy.

Most people worry about a negative self-fulfilling prophecy. This is where you do the opposite of the previous example. You have a fear of a worry, and you think about it a lot. Maybe you prepare for this fear or worry to happen. Then psychologists have argued, you may actually make it happen to yourself. For example, if you are afraid of making an embarrassing mistake during a speech, like at a wedding toast. You write your toast, or speech. You should practice it three times. Then you should try not to think about it, or envision yourself as being a success. If you are afraid of making a mistake, and you worry about it a lot, you may end up making yourself make a mistake.

Was Jesus a crazy man like Charles Manson? Did Jesus have a self fulfilling prophecy? No, because Jesus fulfilled the prophecy from the Old Testament from the books of Isaiah, Elijah, Proverbs, and Psalms. They told of the coming Messiah. The word Christ means Messiah, or chosen one. Jesus was the chosen messenger, and the Son of God. That's why he is called Jesus Christ. Christians and Jews share the Old Testament. The Jewish faith accepts Jesus as a prophet, but not the Jewish Messiah. This is the main reason Christianity and Judaism is different. They share the Old Testament, but Jesus Christ added the New Testament and started Christianity.

Jesus came to make the "bridge", or the cross, between God's world, (the perfect and ideal world, perhaps even a dream world,) and the material world that we live in. Jesus was the messenger, and related to King David. Jesus took the promises, and word of God, and made them real by making miracles, and being sacrificed on the cross to pay for man's sins against God, and then rising from the dead and going to heaven. Jesus was born from a virgin, a miracle birth, because he came from the ideal (the perfect world), to make the ideal of God, (the Word of God) a reality on Earth!

What about faith and reason? Can you have faith in an all powerful and invisible God, and his miracles, and still believe in, or practice science? The answer is yes. Nearly a thousand years ago, there were philosophers that explained how you can believe in God, and practice science. This explanation is called, Scholasticism, and includes the writings of Peter Abelard, and Thomas Aquinas (Summa Theologica). Abelard stated, "By doubting, we come to inquiry, and by inquiring we perceive the truth." (Stearns, Schwartz, Beyer, World History: Traditions and New Directions)

Jason Flick

In essence, science helps explain nature, and religion and philosophy help us give it meaning and purpose. For those that have doubts about faith and religion, there arose a practice of answering questions and answering debates with faith based explanations. This practice is called "apologetics." Science is important, but it cannot explain everything. If you have faith, science explains the material world that we live in, but not the ideal world, or heaven. If science could explain everything, then we would probably have a cure for cancer, and we would extend our lives much longer.

Does science explain everything? Is science perfect? God is perfect. God is the creator of everything. How then, can we even begin to understand God? How can we even comprehend God, when He created us? Some people think that numbers are perfect. For example, a one, is always a one. One and one, are always two. Two and one, are always three. Up to a certain point, this is true. However, people forget that numbers are actually man made creations used to measure "God's" creation. Numbers are tools of measurement.

For example, if you drop a bowling ball and a volleyball from the leaning tower of Pisa (ala Galileo), they both fall at the same rate of acceleration of 3.8 meters per second/per second.
Still, this is NOT going to be the same every time because of varying factors such as wind resistance, etc.

If numbers are always the same, are numbers perfect? Are numbers perfect like God? No, because numbers measure God's creation. God created everything. God created the idea of a circle. God created the circle. Those that believe in divine inspiration, or predestination, would take a step further and argue that God has allowed and inspired (planted the thoughts) of all of our scientific discoveries, and technological accomplishments. What caused Gustave Eiffel to have the inspiration, and the motivation, to build a giant metal tower that is like a curved metal pyramid? Where did this idea come from? Perhaps it came from God.

PROOF OF THE ETERNITY

Science does not explain everything, and science is not perfect. Man made numbers are not perfect. Even though, in theory, numbers are always the same, we can still never perfectly measure the ratio of a circle. The ratio of the circumference of a circle is called "PI." We can use it to closely measure a circle, and it is usually rounded to the number 3.14. But, PI itself, the ratio of a circumference of a circle, actually cannot be measured EXACTLY by numbers!

This is because the actual number of PI goes on forever and ever. PI is proof of eternity.
You can try this yourself. The number PI is found by taking 22 and dividing it by 7. If you take 22 and divide by 7, the number will go on forever. Most calculators will stop at 3.14, or a few further numbers. But, if you find a stronger calculator, or do it manually, it will never end.

PI never ever stops. It goes on forever. So, numbers are NOT perfect because if they were, then we could measure the exact ratio of the circumference of a circle, which we cannot. God is perfect. God created the idea of the circle. God created the circle. Jesus came to make God's word real on Earth. Jesus came to help bridge the gap between us and God.

GOD AND MUSIC

"The devil doesn't stay where there is music."
-Martin Luther
(quote taken from Stearns, Schwartz, Beyer, World History)

If you enjoy numbers and mathematics, and you enjoy numbers, then you should love the Christian Music of composer Johann Sebastian Bach (pronounced Bock). What is music? Music is organized sound. Sound is vibrations in the air. Faster vibrations, like a flute, have a higher pitch and frequency. Slower vibrations, like a tuba, have a lower pitch and frequency. Music takes these vibrations and organizes them into patterns like a mathematic equation. For example, there is the Pythagorean theorem, which is $A2 + B2 = C2$. This is the relationship of the ratio of the sides of a 90 degree, or "right" triangle. This ratio will never change. Music is just like this.

Francis Scott Key composed the Star Spangled Banner (The National Anthem of the United States of America), using an existing pattern of sounds (a melody) that was a tavern drinking song. Today, this musical pattern (melody) is still the same as when he composed it.

Music is created by making patterns of sound (melody). I don't know how or why he composed his music this way, but some of the most complex and mathematical musical patterns were created by Christian Composer, J.S. Bach. His music is very tightly organized like a mathematical equation. It is filled with combinations of different patterns, and then repetitions and variations of those patterns, and then combinations and additions of stacked patterns on top of patterns.

One pattern, or organized system, might be climbing up a scale like a staircase. And one pattern might be descending down a scale like walking down a staircase. Then he combines these two patterns at the same time, and it is like turning math into music. His music is like math because it is filled with organized and symmetrical ratios and relationships of sound. These ratios, or relationships, are called "chords."

Can you see God in numbers? I cannot. But numbers are representations, and ideal, similar to God the creator. Can you hear God in music? Music is based on ideal organized relationships of sound. It is not real until you play it, or sing it.

In this way, Jesus is like music. Music exists, whether you play it or not. Just like God exists whether you believe in him, or not. Jesus is like music, because he took the message of God, and made it real in the material world. Just like Bach wrote organized patterns of music on paper to make his music real.

Can you hear God in music? Bach thought so. How did he do it? Where did his music come from? Maybe it was inspired by God. Maybe that's why we sing and play music in church, like Jesus Christ, it brings us closer to God.

DAY SIX: TUESDAY: APRIL FOOL'S DAY

FEATHER IN MY CAP

Jason Flick

#48: GOVERNMENT: APRIL FOOL'S DAY

(1)
Today's April Fool's
I don't know who the fool is?
Me, or the government?

(2)
I'm unhappy though.
My probation was too long.
But, today's last day!

(3)
I'm so excited.
It feels good to be alive.
But, I'm nervous too.

(4)
Today's my last meet,
With probation officer.
Then, I'm a free man.

(5)
Free to be a… jerk.
Free to go to the strip clubs.
And, free to not tip.

(6)
But, I'm just kidding.
Probably nothing will change.
I hope for better.

(7)
Pot is now legal,
In some of the other states.
But, I think I'll pass.

Haiku Holiday

(8)
But, now I can go,
To Canada for Cubans;
And, Mexico too.

(9)
I've been hiding out;
That's why Haiku Holiday.
Finishing my time.

(10)
I'm looking forward,
To bigger and better things.
I can teach again!

(11)
Well, wish me good luck.
I've got my suit and tie on,
And, I brushed my teeth.

(12)
Later, the same day…
God Damn Stinking Son of Bitch!
Fucking Shit Bastard!

(13)
Piss Shit Fuck Cock Balls!
I… did not get to go free.
Had drug test and fine.

(14)
I still have to wait.
I was afraid this might pass.
I prepared, in case.

(15)
Cigars might have hemp.
Some, might have it, anyway.
So, I drank a lot.

(16)
Taking drug tests, sucks.
You have to pee in a cup,
While someone watches.

(17)
My bladder's quite mean.
It only works at bad times;
Church, the movies… sex.

(18)
Even with gallons,
It's hard to pee on command.
I tried to prepare.

(19)
Stopped smoking cigars,
It was yesterday, I think.
And, I drank water.

(20)
It might be a myth.
But, drinking green tea can help,
To clean out system.

(21)
A cop told me that.
So, he may have been lying.
I have formula.

(22)
It's vitamin beer.
It's Blue Moon Belgian White Ale.
Blue Moon Brewing Co.

(23)
The can is all blue.
With orange, coriander,
It tastes delicious.

(24)
But, I add some stuff.
I mix it with Gatorade,
And, vitamins too.

(25)
Effervescent tabs;
They fizz and dissolve in drink,
Like, Alka-Seltzer.

(26)
I like to eat them.
They're like vitamin candy.
Now, I sit and wait.

(27)
This April Fool's Day,
It looks like I am the fool…
Now, I'll smoke cigars.

THE AMERICAN BRAIN WASHING MACHINE

"Pretty sneaky sis!"
-Milton Bradley
1980's television commercial for the game, "battleship, or connect four?"

Americans invented television. Television is paid for by advertisers. Advertisers want people to watch television so that they will watch commercials, and buy their products. The more people that watch a t.v. program, the more money they can charge advertisers to sell their stuff on commercials.

When is the cheapest time to advertise? At, 3:00 in the morning. Why, because no one is watching (except me). The problem is that the t.v. people are making t.v. shows to get people to watch. The more people that watch their show, the more money that they can make. So, the t.v. people are making shows that will do anything to get people to watch. As a result, the t.v. people are making t.v. shows that are increasingly more violent and sexually explicit!

Some people believe that is is bad for society. Some people believe that advertisers and television shows try to program popular behavior by showing examples of how you should live. This is called, "social engineering."

This is because some people believe in the idea that... "monkey see, monkey do." Are you a monkey? Does this concept apply to society? I do not know if the idea of "monkey see, monkey do" is true, and I don't know if television will brainwash you. I do know that television and advertising is a powerful form of communication. Television advertising is so powerful, that I can remember a t.v. ad punch line like, "pretty sneaky sis." from more than 2 decades past.

In summary, the bad news is that t.v. will probably only get more and more shocking! Television will probably continue to get more and more violent and sexually explicit. This is because, just like taking drugs, the more we watch, the more tolerance we build. We, the viewers, and society, become "desensitized" to the graphic situations. Then the t.v. people try to make shows even more shocking to keep our attention. We become, "desensitized" to the violence and sexual content on t.v. Jesus Christ would say that "our hearts become hardened."
Perhaps, this results in people becoming more cynical and negative?

The ironic good news, is that with modern technology, such as dvr recorders, vcr's, dvd's, and cable, and dish television, a person has more television and entertainment options to choose from. This is ironic, because it both allows viewers non-graphic programs as an option to watch if they want, but at the same time, it increases the competition of the t.v. people and creates a motivation to make even dirtier and sexier shows.

Don't get me wrong. I thank God for television and entertainment. I love t.v. and I watch all kinds of television. However, I am concerned about how t.v. programs have become more cynical and negative in my opinion.

Haiku Holiday

This is… one reason why I wrote this "smutty" and "filthy" Christian book. I am attempting to combat the cynical messages of the modern media, and do whatever it takes to shock people to get them to read the "Good News" of the Gospel of Jesus Christ.

Basically, I don't care if you watch t.v. Don't stop watching t.v. I watch t.v. But, don't forget about the positive and hopeful messages from God, sent by his only son, Jesus Christ, who died on the cross, as a sacrifice to pay for and forgive your sins if you accept him as your lord and savior.

So, I have written this dirty book, to get you to read about the positive messages of hope from Jesus Christ. "Pretty sneaky sis!"

#49: SLAVERY: T.V. TIME

(1)
Hey everybody,
It's time for television!
t.v. time is great!

(2)
I would like to know,
Who first used the initials,
t.v. for the word?

(3)
I love to watch it.
Especially the movies;
Sunday afternoon.

(4)
There's the news program.
There's late night television.
There's prime time t.v.

Jason Flick

(5)
There's the soap operas.
A new story every day.
And, of course there's sports.

(6)
There's something for all.
My favorites are the sit-coms.
Scripted comedy.

(7)
Some shows provide hope.
They give escape from problems.
Fantasy that's real.

(8)
During ancient Greece,
Comedies and tragedies,
Were performed outdoors.

(9)
The ancient romans,
Had the coliseum filled,
For gladiators.

(10)
In medieval times,
There were court jesters with songs,
And, some dancers too.

(9)
Shakespearian times,
Had poetic plays on stage,
At "Globe Theater."

(10)
First Americans,
Watched traveling vaudeville shows,
And, there's the circus.

Haiku Holiday

(11)
Now, it's on t.v.
You can watch it all for free.
You need a t.v.

(12)
Electricity
Brings all the magic to be.
When you watch… t.v.

(14)
There's education,
With public television,
You can watch, and learn!

(15)
Great when you're alone.
Or, in the hospital sick.
Or, when killing time.

(16)
But, please be careful.
It can become addictive.
And, it will steal time.

(17)
It's a temptation,
When you have homework to do,
Or, there's chores around.

(18)
Just like alcohol,
Or smoking cigars, and such,
Don't become a slave.

(19)
Sometimes, I feel like,
I'm a slave to all of these.
So then, I cut back.

(20)
I try to make plans.
I pick my favorite programs;
A t.v. diet.

(21)
I record the shows,
That I really want to watch.
Then, I don't waste time.

(22)
Too much anything,
Can eventually harm you,
Or make you a slave.

(23)
You could read a book.
You could play a game with friends.
You could take a walk.

(24)
Too much t.v. ads,
And watching too much t.v.
Will make you go blind.

(25)
Perhaps you should know.
This message is not for you.
I'm talking to... me.

(26)
You could masterbate!
But, not while watching t.v.
Don't eat your t.v.

#50: SENSE: BEER AND BUNS

(1)
It's called "Steel Reserve."
Double the ingredients,
Double the brewing.

(2)
The "Steel Brewing Co."
It's "High Gravity" lager.
Eight point one percent.

(3)
Try some by itself!
24 fluid ounces...
One pint, 8 ounces.

(4)
That's the size and weight,
Of my penis... on the moon,
With NO gravity.

(5)
That's a double beer,
With double ingredients!
It tastes smooth and sweet.

(6)
Marked, two eleven...
That's the medieval symbol,
That was used for... STEEL!

(7)
Like an ancient beer,
It's got a beautiful glow;
Call it liquid bread.

(8)
Everybody loves…
The smell of cinnamon buns.
Beer and buns are great!

(9)
Cinnamon and beer,
Make a nice combination.
I say, "Spice is nice!"

(10)
Take one tablespoon,
And fill it with cinnamon.
Dump it in a mug.

(11)
Then pour in the beer.
It looks like sandy chocolate…
A foamy "beer shake!"

(12)
Cinnamon is good;
Speeds up metabolism…
It's good for your heart!

(13)
A "heart healthy" beer?
It makes a good breakfast drink,
Or a nice dessert.

(14)
Cinnamon and spice,
And beer that is really nice;
That's what gets girls drunk!

(15)
Oooh that's a nice buzz!
You can try different amounts.
Sometimes… less is more.

JEAN PAUL SARTRE

"A poor God-damned soldier has no opinions... And prisoners even less," he answered dryly. "Everything is asking us for our opinion. Everything! We are encircled by questions: the whole thing's a farce. Questions are asked of us as though we were men, as though somebody to make us believe we still are men. But no. No. No. What a farce, this shadow of a question put by the shadow of a war to a handful of make-believe men!"

"What's the use of having an opinion? You're not going to decide."

> He stopped talking. He thought suddenly: life has got to go on. Day after day we have got to gather in the rotten fruit of defeat, to work out in a world that has gone to pieces that total choice I have just refused to make. But, good God! I didn't choose this war, nor this defeat; by what phony trick must I assume responsibility for them... "We have nothing to do with this mess!"

-Jean Paul Sartre, Troubled Sleep, p.59

I too, find myself fighting a battle. A much less significant battle, however. Not a life or death "Battle of the Bulge..." but a "Battle of the Bills!" I am struggling currently to make ends meet, as a student, and an independent writer.

I just received notice in the mail that my "unemployment insurance" claim has been denied... again, because they don't believe that I'm a student. Also, my electric bill is due, and I just received notice they are threatening to turn off my power because I am a week late on my bill (and, I don't have it!) Also, I have received notice that my storage locker will be confiscated in one week if I don't pay up. But, that gives me a week to move my stuff out. And, I just received a bill for another hundred dollars to renew my license plate. But, I should be okay there, because I am trying to sell that car anyway. Still, for now, I am not in danger of losing life or limb like soldiers sometimes are. And, for now, and for today, I have a refrigerator. And, it is stocked with... bread, peanut butter, jelly... and beer, and even soda... and vodka... and chocolate.

Jason Flick

I have… a roof over my head. Thus, as I currently struggle to make ends meet, I follow the ideals of the famous folk song and live… "Day by Day." I find inspiration in The Lord's Prayer, that states, "Give us this day our daily bread." In other words, help us to get through this day. It is perhaps ironic, then, that Jean Paul Sartre, who is credited as an advocate for existentialism, seems to say the same thing in this previous passage from his book, Troubled Sleep, that the Lord's Prayer does (found in Matthew, 6:9 of The New Testament).

#51: WAR AND PEACE: SARTRE SAYS…

(1)
Sartre says… You Suck!
What you going to do bout it?
I'm Jean Paul Sartre

Post Script: Sartre is pronounced Sart-trah.

THE LORD SAID

Here is a short poem that is not a haiku. This is paraphrased from the Bible.

THE LORD SAID

The Lord said,
"Revolutions come, And politicians go.
But there's only one thing,
That you need to know.

The rain will fall,
And the wind will blow.
But, I will always love you,
From your head to your toe."

#52: NATURE: ICE TEA BEER

(1)
Plank Road Brewery
Brews since 1855
This beer is "Ice House."

(2)
It's from Milwaukee;
Brewed with ice, below freezing.
The can is ice cold!

(3)
Five point five percent,
A respectable level...
For a "cheese head" beer.

(4)
The can is silver,
Along with white, blue, and grey.
The "Yankee" colors!

(5)
The can looks like ice.
It has a medium taste;
Not too light, or dark.

(6)
It is creamy smooth.
It's one of my favorites.
I could drink it straight.

(7)
It has a story.
I am making this part up...
But, I think it's true.

(8)
Back in the old days,
Before refrigerators,
One used an "ice box."

(9)
They cut blocks of ice,
From out of Lake Michigan,
Took them to "Ice House."

(10)
Surrounded by bricks,
The Ice stayed cold all summer,
And people bought it.

(11)
It was delivered,
By trucks, to people's houses.
Just like… the "milk man."

(12)
What is a milk man?
Well, there's more than one meaning.
That's another tale.

(13)
Milk men "delivered."
They would bring milk to your house…
And… "satisfied" wives.

(14)
Ice house makes good tea.
You can make iced tea with beer.
Any beer will do.

(15)
I make peppermint;
3 bags for 15 minutes,
To a half hour.

(16)
You can add others,
Such as damiana tea.
That's for… libido.

(17)
It's called "sexy tea.
Then, add a shot of vodka,
To make "extra" fun.

(18)
It's food for picnics,
When you spread the table cloth…
And you're a milkman.

MARK TWAIN

"The moment he was gone, she ran to a closet and got out the ruin of a jacket which Tom had gone pirating in. Then she stopped, with it in her hand, and said to herself:

"No, I don't dare. Poor boy, I reckon he's lied about it- but it's a blessed, blessed lie, There's such comfort come from it. I hope the Lord- I know the Lord will forgive him, because it was such good-heartedness in him to tell it. But I don't want to find out it's a lie. I won't look."

She put the jacket away, and stood by musing a minute. Twice she put out her hand to take the garment again, and twice she refrained. Once more she ventured and this time she fortified herself with the thought:

"It's a good lie- it's a good lie- I won't let it grieve me."

So she sought the jacket pocket. A moment later she was reading Tom's piece of bark through flowing tears and saying:

"I could forgive the boy, now, if he's committed a million sins!"
-Mark Twain, The Adventures of Tom Sawyer, p. 130.

Jason Flick

This excerpt from Mark Twain's American classic, Tom Sawyer, is about a crisis of faith. The lady thought Tom was lying. She couldn't believe that he was telling the truth. She had to verify it for herself. It turned out that Tom WAS telling the truth, even though it was hard to believe.

I think that there are three kinds of stories. There are [A]: stories that are wild, and hard to believe, but still true. There are [B]: stories that are true, but exaggerated and embellished.
And there are [C]: stories that are concocted and invented, but with a purpose (such as education, or entertainment).

The world is filled with lies and deceptions. The name Mark Twain itself is a "pseudonym" or fake name. Mark Twain's real name was Samuel Clemens. Sometimes lies are the truth, and the truth is a lie. The name Mark Twain is an invented lie, it was not Samuel Clemens real name. But, that was the name he chose, so it became his real name.

Sometimes wars are started for reasons that are not real. Sometimes governments make rules and laws for different reasons than they say. You cannot always trust what is on the news. Sometimes the news is a lie. And, sometimes a lie… is the truth. Sometimes a hero is also a villain. Sometimes a villain, can be a hero.

Socrates was sentenced to death, because he preached seeking the truth, and it scared the people in power (the government). Jesus was sentenced to death also, partly, because he was preaching the truth about God's word and about the world. People do not always like to hear the truth.

Jesus himself, was accused of being a villain in the start of his ministry, because people were afraid to hear the truth. After Jesus was baptized and received the holy spirit, he would preach the word of God, and heal people and do miracles. These miracles frightened people, and they thought that he was the devil. They thought that Jesus was a villain because he told the truth.

Is The Holy Bible, (The Old Testament, and The New Testament), real? Or is it just a bunch of made up stories? This is a cold and hard question. The Holy Bible is real because it exists. It was even the first mass produced book ever printed by the Guttenberg printing press. It was written and created by somebody.

Are the stories real, or are they made up? This is a question that most Christians will ask themselves, or be asked by someone sometime in their life. It is only natural to have doubts, even if you are a faithful Christian. Are the stories real, or are they made up? You have to decide for yourself.

Millions of people before you have gone to church and believed The Holy Bible to be true. It's generally accepted as true, by historians, that Jesus of Nazareth was real and existed. Jesus Christ had a ministry and dedicated followers that were willing to die for their faith. He was really crucified, and died as a political prisoner and criminal. Can you believe that this is true?

There are other historical people that have been political prisoners and sentenced to death, so it is possible. Do you believe that the American revolutionary, Patrick Henry, was executed by the British because he was an American patriot? Do you believe that Joan of Arc was captured by the English, and burned at the stake, both because she was a woman in power, and a leader of the French?

Everyone has doubts about their religious philosophy. This is natural. Anyone that has religious faith has likely had religious doubts. Even in The New Testament, there is a message to show how having doubts is natural. One of the disciples (followers) of Jesus, named Thomas, said that he would not believe that Jesus had risen from the grave unless he could see it for himself, and see the nail holes in his hands and feet. Then, Jesus appeared to him to show him that it is real, and that he rose from the dead. Jesus appeared to him to give him faith so that he could tell others about Jesus. This follower of Jesus Christ, came to be known as "doubting Thomas." If Jesus was a real person, and had real followers (that's how we know about him today), then it's possible that one of his followers was named Thomas, and had doubts about his teachings. Certainly you can believe that this is possible?

Is the Bible just made up stories? How do you get faith in God, The Holy Bible, and Jesus Christ? You have to try to believe it. If you try to believe it, then it will become real to you. It will become real to you, and Christianity will bring you joy, and comfort, and salvation and forgiveness from your sins, and help you to get to know God, and go to heaven in the afterlife.

Can you believe that there was a real man named Jesus of Nazareth that lived in Israel more than 2000 years ago? If you go to Jerusalem today, parts of the original city are still preserved just as they were 2000 years ago. You can see and touch the original walls of the city gates from 2000 years ago, and know that Jerusalem is a real place and existed 2000 years ago.
I have been there, and seen it, and touched the walls. I know that Jerusalem is real.

Can you believe that others followed Jesus Christ, and believed in him. And, today, there are still people that believe in Jesus Christ and worship Jesus Christ as the Son of God? As I write this, I believe and worship Jesus Christ.

Can you believe that people build entire buildings as monuments to God, and to Jesus Christ? In every town in America, there is usually at least one Christian Church, or one nearby. These churches were built and used by people that believe and worship Jesus Christ. And, there are Christian churches just like this all over the world.

In Europe, there is even an entire city that exists to worship Jesus Christ. This is the Vatican City, in Rome, and it is the headquarters of the Roman Catholic Church, and the home to the Roman Catholic Pope (the leader of the Catholic Church). If you are in America, you can go to one of these Christian Church buildings and see that they are real. They will almost always be open and used for worship on any Sunday morning.

Do you believe in ghosts? Do you believe in the possibility of ghosts? If you believe in, or are scared of ghosts, then you believe in an afterlife. If you believe in an afterlife, and in the possibility of ghosts, then you can believe in the possibility of God sending a ghost messenger called The Holy Spirit, or The Holy Ghost to guide and inspire people, and to do miracles. If you can believe in ghosts, then you can believe in angels, which are like ghosts that serve God, and come to earth to do his work. If you can believe in ghosts and angels, then you can believe that Jesus Christ talked to God, The Holy Ghost, and angels, and that he did miracles with their help, and that he rose from the dead as a miracle to show us that God is real.

Can you believe in yourself and that you are real? Yes, you know that you are real because you are reading this now, and because you are experiencing life. You can see and touch and taste and smell, and walk, and talk, or at least do some of those things. You know that you are alive now. What will happen next? Are you going to grow older, and one day die?

Most people will experience having a family member, or friend die. When this happens, they are alive one day, and then they stop living and existing as we know it. Then they are gone from our life. We can see children younger than us (maybe neighbors, or relatives, or your own children) grow and get bigger, older, and smarter. And, we can see older people (maybe neighbors, relatives, or friends) that have grown and matured. They might be walking on the street, or at a restaurant. They might have lost their hair, or their hair may have turned grey, and they may move slower, and they may have wrinkled skin. This is because they have lived longer, and aged.

You know then, that you were born, and you have grown older, bigger, and smarter. You are probably taller and bigger now, and you probably have your memories of being a child. You know that you will probably continue to grow older, and eventually you will probably die. What do you think will happen after you die? What happens when we die? Is there an afterlife? Is there life after death? Is there another spiritual existence after our body dies on Earth?

Do you think that it is possible that there is another existence after you die on Earth? What will happen to you when you die? Do you think that when you die, you end, and you stop existing? Can you believe that there is another existence after you die?

Jason Flick

What happens every night? Every night, most people go to sleep for around eight hours. What do we do when we sleep? It is like we are dead. We lay down, and we close our eyes, and we stop moving and talking. We do not die when we sleep. We still breathe and our heart beats. But we are not actively alert. However, we still think. This thinking is called dreaming.

When you dream, it will feel like you are doing things, but they are not real. You might dream that you are on vacation, but you are actually sleeping at home in your bed. Are dreams real? Have you ever had a dream? Can you believe that dreams exist? Do you believe that you go to sleep, and then wake up again the next day? Most people experience sleep, dreams, and waking up and starting a new day. If you believe that you sleep and dream, but are still alive, and then wake up again, can you believe that there might be another existence for you after your life on Earth? Isn't life on earth, maybe just like a dream? Maybe when you die… you begin a new existence, or a new life?

What about miracles, angels, the after-life, and transformation? Jesus says that in the after-life, we will be like the angels. I find it easy to believe in an all powerful creator God that created all the creatures of the world. There is so much variety in animals, and in people, and in the way nature works, that it is all to amazing to me to think that it could all be accidental, or coincidental. I do not know if the world was created in seven days. Perhaps when the Bible says the world was created in seven of "God's" days, which could be 7000 years to us?

Last night, I had a fly land on my hand. It surprised me, because I did not even know that it was there. It existed, and I did not even know it. I looked down, and there was a really big housefly on my hand. Then I waved the fly away. Then, I watched that fly… fly away, and I thought about it's' existence. Here is a tiny fly that exists without my knowledge in my house. It can fly through the air, and it eats dust. This fly will probably only live for about a month of my time. That is a short time to me. But, to the fly, one month is an entire lifetime. Can you imagine an all powerful creator that created everything on Earth, and how short our lives are in comparison?

What about evolution? Much of evolution and natural selection seems to make sense, and it does explain a lot of nature. But, I still don't think that it explains everything. And, even if there is evolution in God's creature's, could this not be part of the plan and creation of a creator God?

What about transformation, and life after death? Isn't it possible that when we die, we are changed, and transform into another existence? Take the amazing example of the butterfly.
This creature is born and lives as a small furry caterpillar. A cute little fuzzy and slow insect that crawls on the earth and eats grass. Then, this creature, makes a change called "metamorphosis." It creates a "cocoon", or a sleeping chamber, and then it goes to sleep and changes. When it wakes up, it is a completely new creature with wings, and it flies instead of walking, and… it has beautiful wings. How is it possible that a creature can change from one thing to another by itself?

If there is a God that created everything, then you can believe Christianity might be true, and that God sent his son as a messenger for us. If you believe that there are unexplainable things in the world that we can't understand, then you can believe in miracles.

Yes, we can discover and explain things with science, but that doesn't mean that we can understand them. If you can believe that God created us and loves us, then you can believe that he gave us knowledge and the ability to think and understand things, perhaps so that we can know him better.

It is true that there are lies in the world, and that people lie. But it's also true that sometimes people tell the truth. And, sometimes the truth is hard to believe. Take paper currency, for example. Everyone in modern society uses money to buy and sell things.
But, it's still just a piece of paper. Still, we will give away our possessions, time, and work, to trade for this paper. You believe that this special paper called, "money" will allow you to buy and sell things don't you? And yet, it is… just a piece of paper.

Can you believe that Christianity is true? You know that there are others that believe it is true. You know that it is true that the Bible exists. Historians know that a man named Jesus from Nazareth existed, and had a ministry, and followers. The excerpt from Mark Twain's Tom Sawyer showed a woman that could not believe that Tom was telling the truth about where he had been, and what he had done. But, even though she thought it was a lie, and she did not believe it, when she investigated his story, it was the truth!

There are three kinds of stories. The stories that [A], are wild and hard to believe but true. The stories that [B] are true but exaggerated and embellished. And, the stories that [C] are invented, but with a purpose. Is Christianity true? You have to decide for yourself. God sent the messenger and gave you the freedom to choose. But, I believe the Bible is true, and that Jesus Christ is the Son of God. And, I think that it is worth your consideration to think about.

#53: TRUTH: SAWYER'S SERENDIPITY

(1)
We have all told lies.
But, we have all told the truth.
Sometimes, we fear truth.

(2)
God is so awesome,
That it can be easier,
To deny his truth.

(3)
Tom Sawyer told lies.
But, he also told the truth!
The truth can be hard.

(4)
Just a little faith,
Can change your life forever,
And reveal God's plan.

#54: CHANGE: SIREN SWAN

(1)
There is a creature,
That makes a transformation;
A magical change.

(2)
It starts as a duck,
A small and modest brown bird.
Then it makes a change.

(3)
It becomes a swan;
A glorious big white bird,
That shines with beauty.

(4)
Is this just like man?
A creature walking the Earth;
Changed and freed at death?

Post Script: Jesus says that God's forgiveness is a free gift from God. He wants you to live a good life. I am not suicidal. Suicide is a sin and a terrible insult against God, and those that know you. Even though I believe death is a metamorphosis, your life is a beautiful gift from god and should be lived to the fullest. We all go through ups and downs in life. We all face trouble. That is why Jesus gave us the message of hope for the afterlife, and the gift of dreams. If you have thoughts of harming yourself or others, please say a prayer immediately, and contact a local hospital. Try this prayer:

EMERGENCY PRAYER

Help me Jesus.
Forgive me for evil thoughts.
Clear my mind of evil thoughts.
Give me peace.
Praise God.
Amen.

DAY SEVEN: WEDNESDAY

BED HEAD

#55: ANIMAL: PET MY PET SNAKE

(1)
Why are snakes so bad?
There are some poisonous snakes.
There's the rattle snake.

(2)
There's the poison asp.
There's the serpent from the tree...
With forbidden fruit.

(3)
It's now apparent...
Forbidden fruit... is INCEST!
Eve came... from Adam!

(4)
I'm speculating.
Did Adam look like Eve then?
There were no mirrors.

(5)
Devil was serpent.
It does not say what kind though?
Perhaps a lizard?

(6)
I had a lizard;
A pet iguana named "Spike.
I gave him away.

(7)
There's the famed python,
It strangles its prey, and eats;
Much used... by strippers.

(8)
But, the most famed snake,
The snake that snake charmers use,
That's the King Cobra!

(9)
King Cobra's a beer.
It's "premium malt liquor."
It has a "smooth taste."

(10)
The Snake's Mid-Western.
King Cobra's from Missouri,
From Anheuser Busch.

(11)
It's 40 ounces!
Who really cares about taste?
It's less than 2 bucks!

(12)
A black and red snake.
A 40 ounce glass of beer.
That's a big bottle!

(13)
And, when you're thirsty,
It tastes like… forbidden fruit;
So salty, and wet.

(14)
40 ounce bottle!
That's three and a third cans beer!
That's a lot of beer.

(15)
With 3 point 3 beers,
You can make macaroni…
And still get a buzz!

(16)
Turn it bottom up!
I'm talking about the beer.
The snake is a two.

(17)
Two is the wild card.
It will mix with any group.
Two will make a win!

(18)
When God cloned Adam,
Did taking a rib hurt him?
Still, Adam was pleased.

(19)
Eve came from Adam.
And, they probably had sex.
First masturbation?

(20)
When you go shopping,
And you take your girlfriend with.
Say… "I'll get produce!"

#56: KNOWLEDGE: FORBIDDEN FEAST

(1)
Knowledge can kill you!
If you have too much knowledge,
Or, have the wrong kind.

(2)
If you are a spy…
"We have ways… to make you talk!"
That's in the movies.

Jason Flick

(3)
Once you learn something,
It can be hard to forget.
THINK… before you… think!

(4)
I'm talking about…
Bible's book of Genesis.
Adam and Eve Fell.

(5)
They had paradise.
God gave them only one rule.
Don't eat the bad fruit.

(6)
The fruit was knowledge.
It took them away from God,
Because they gained pride.

(7)
Knowledge is power.
Power can lead to bragging.
How much is too much?

(8)
Man keeps learning more.
Man is proud of achievements.
But, we forget God.

(9)
God is the power.
God provides the resources.
God grants us all things.

(10)
Because of knowledge,
We are proud of our makings.
And, we forget God.

(11)
What is secret fruit?
It does not say, what it is?
The fruit of knowledge.

(12)
Some say, it was figs.
Some say, it might have been peaches.
The peach pit's poison.

(13)
I say, tomatoes!
Both fruit... AND vegetable!
Bi-sexual food?

(14)
The forbidden feast,
Is Beer, cheese, macaroni,
And tomato soup.

(15)
It's not really bad.
It's fast, cheap, easy pleasure.
Just like... my dream girl.

(16)
Too much anything...
Is going to be bad for you.
Moderation's key!

(17)
Were Adam and Eve,
Real people in paradise?
They may have been real.

(18)
The important thing,
The lesson to learn is real.
Temptations exist.

(19)
It is important.
Not to forget about, God.
The maker of all.

FORBIDDEN FEAST RECIPE

BEER MACARONI AND CHEESE... AND TOMATO SOUP

Ingredients:
1 cup beer (King Cobra, or Magnum Malt Liquor)
1 can condensed tomato soup (11 oz?)
1 box macaroni and cheese
2 onions
1 stick of butter or margarine (½ cup/ 8 tablespoons)
1 tea spoon pepper
2 tablespoons garlic powder
1 teaspoon garlic powder
1 teaspoon onion powder
3 tablespoons parsley
1 tablespoon sugar
3 tablespoons parmesan cheese

Directions:

Part 1:
1. Pour 1 cup of beer into pot and let sit.

Part 2:
2. Take 2 onions and chop ends off. Peel onions and rinse. Then cut onions into quarters. Slice onions into ½ inch and ½ inch pieces.
3. Put chopped onions in a microwave safe bowl.
4. Take ½ stick of butter or margarine (4 tablespoons/ ¼ cup), and cut into ¼ inch slices.
5. Add the butter slices to the bowl of onions.
6. Add 1 tablespoon of garlic powder and stir.
7. Place bowl of chopped onions in microwave for 2 minutes. Make sure the butter is melted, and stir.

Part 3:
8. Put pot of beer on stove on high for 2 minutes. Beer will bubble up. Stir until it boils.
9. Open the box of macaroni and remove the powder cheese packet. Pour the macaroni noodles into the pot and stir.
10. Add 1 teaspoon of pepper and stir.
11. Add 1 tablespoon of parsley and stir.
12. Add 1 teaspoon of garlic powder and stir.
13. Add the heated onions and garlic butter and stir.
14. Continue to heat and stir for 3 to 5 minutes.
15. Remove pot from the stove and set on a plate to let cool.

Part 4:
16. Add a splash of beer and stir.
17. Take the cheese powder packet and shake before opening to remove clumps.
18. Open cheese powder and stir into pot.
19. Stir and let cool. Add a splash of beer to help mix the cheese powder.
20. Add 1 tablespoon of parsley and stir.

Part 5:
21. Open a can of condensed tomato soup and add to pot and stir.
22. Add 1 tablespoon of sugar and stir.
23. Add 1 teaspoon of onion powder and stir.
24. Take ½ stick of butter or margarine and cut into ¼ inch slices. Add butter to pot and stir.
25. Add 1 tablespoon garlic powder and stir.
26. Put pot on stove. Heat on high for 3 to 5 minutes and stir until it begins to boil.
27. Remove pot from heat and place on plate to cool. Add 1 tablespoon parsley and stir.
28. Add 3 tablespoons of parmesan cheese and stir.
29. Let cool for 5 to 10 minutes.
30. Serve in 3 or 4 bowls. Add 1 tablespoon of parmesan cheese to each bowl to dust the top.

Addendum: I actually like this dish served cold. You can put it in the fridge for a couple of days, and it tastes great cold, or as a topping for a sandwich, or on crackers for a snack.

Post Script: Other than carbs and butter, there is nothing wrong or forbidden about this plate... unless you substitute cannabis for parsley. Which you should not do... It's forbidden (kind of). Enjoy.

Post Script II: In all sincerity, I smoke cigars, but not cannabis, and I don't know if those parsley measurements are acceptable. If substituting cannabis, maybe try half that amount. Personally, I would rather double the beer.

#57: DUTY: CLEANLINESS IS GODLINESS... SOMETIMES

(1)
I waited all week,
To write this special haiku,
Avoiding... dishes!

(2)
Time to do dishes.
I let them sit all week long.
Now, I'm out of them.

(3)
No more clean dishes.
I can't afford paper plates...
I probably can.

(4)
I like to eat food.
It tastes better on dishes.
Paper plates... are gross.

(5)
Time for my duty.
It's an honor, AND duty…
To clean the dishes.

(6)
Why did I wait so?
That's my favorite invention…
Dishwashing machine.

(7)
But, obviously…
I don't have a dishwasher.
I do them by hand.

(8)
I have the supplies.
You need dishwashing liquid.
There are different scents.

(9)
Grapefruit is the best;
Or, antibacterial…
Apple, or lemon.

(10)
You need a dish brush.
There's a sponge on a handle,
With liquid inside.

(11)
I prefer the brush.
It helps to scrape off the chunks.
It lasts… forever.

(12)
Most importantly,
You have to have hot water.
Then, they're shiny clean.

(13)
Mugs… are IMPORTANT!
I put them in the freezer,
For an ice cold beer!

(14)
Some people soak them.
But, they ALWAYS forget them.
They get all slimy.

(15)
I'd like to toss them.
If I win the lottery…
I'll just… buy new ones.

(16)
I have a washer…
A washing machine for clothes.
What would happen if???

#58: SPACE: THE SALT OF THE SEA

(1)
There's a special place;
Home to the fountain of youth,
Discovered by Spain.

(2)
Juan Ponce de Leon,
Found it 1517…
Looking for bathroom.

(3)
It's name means flowers.
It's home of "Magic Kingdom."
Home of the "Gators"

(4)
There's alligators.
They are like small dinosaurs.
They'll eat you alive.

(5)
Just like… a "land shark,"
But, without the "Jaws" music.
They're fast and sneaky!

(6)
This magical land,
Filled with tourists and fishing,
Is called… Florida.

(7)
There's "Landshark Lager;"
Margaritaville Brewing,
Brewed in Jacksonville.

(8)
The real fun is found…
Down in the Florida Keys.
There's treasure and fish!

(9)
The Florida Keys;
One Hundred and Fifty Miles;
A chain of islands.

(10)
They're all connected.
You can drive on a long bridge.
Key West's the last one.

(11)
It's the most South part,
Found in the united states.
It's like a "Mecca"

(12)
Somewhere you should go,
At least one time in your life.
So many flowers.

(13)
Ernest Hemingway,
Lived in a Key West Estate,
With a swimming pool.

(14)
"Ernesto" had cats.
He was "Papa" Hemingway,
With dozens of cats.

(15)
I tried to steal one.
There's one that looks just like him.
But then, it bit me.

(16)
That's how I wrote this.
It gave me magic powers.
Ernest's special cat!

(17)
I just made that up.
But, it's a wonderful place,
Sea salt in the air.

(18)
The Isle of Key West,
It's like a different country…
But, American.

(19)
Ernest went fishing;
Wrote, "The Old Man and The Sea."
People like to fish.

(20)
Jesus liked to fish.
He said, be "fishers of men."
But, he caught fish too.

(21)
Jesus took a fish,
And used it for a symbol.
The Christian "Ichthys"

(22)
I suck at fishing.
But, I love being at sea.
There is so much space.

SALSA OF THE SEA

Here is an awesome and easy snack that is reminiscent of hanging out in Key West, or any other sea side stand. You can eat this with any crackers and chips, and it's healthy. I recommend salt-free saltine crackers, because they are healthy and cheap. And… don't forget the beer.

Ingredients:
1 can tuna
1 onion
1 tablespoon garlic powder
1 tablespoon dried parsley
4 tablespoons beer (or more)
3 tablespoons of parmesan cheese
3 tablespoons of ketchup
1 tablespoon of mustard
Extra ingredients (optional):
1 tablespoon of cilantro, or coriander (optional)
1 slice of lime, or orange (optional)

This recipe is so easy and fast. And, it's pretty healthy, and tasty too.

Directions:

1. Open a can of tuna, drain the water, and pour into a bowl.
2. Wash an onion and chop off the ends. Peel off the outside layer. Cut in half from top to bottom. Then slice each half into horizontal slices, and then chop those slices into ¼, and ½ inch pieces. Then add chopped onions to the bowl of tuna.
3. Add 1 tablespoon of garlic powder, and stir with a fork.
4. Add 1 tablespoon of dried parsley, and stir with a fork.
5. Add 4 tablespoons of beer (you can add more later), and stir with a fork.
6. Add 3 tablespoons of parmesan cheese, and stir with a fork.
7. Add 3 tablespoons of ketchup, and stir with a fork.
8. Add 1 tablespoon of mustard, and stir with a fork.
9. Extra option: add 1 tablespoon of cilantro or coriander, and stir, then squeeze a slice of lime, or an orange slice.

Voila! Eat with crackers or chips. No cooking necessary. Refrigerate when done.

CHRISTIANITY PART II

(1) How do I become a Christian? What do I do?
(2) Who is Jesus Christ?
(3) Why should I become a Christian?

How do you become a Christian? It's simple. You just accept Jesus Christ as your Lord and Savior, accept his forgiveness of your sins, and believe in him as the Son of God. What do you do? You can start by picking a church and going to church.

There are a lot of different Christian churches. Each one is a little different, and will say you need to do different things. Baptist Christian Churches will way you need to have a public baptism as an adult. Roman Catholic Christian Churches will say you need to join the Catholic Church, and confess your sins to a priest, and acknowledge the Pope in Rome as God's authority on Earth. Protestant Churches such as the Anglican Church, Episcopalian

Church, Lutheran Church, and Methodist Church, will say that you pray and confess your sins directly to Jesus. Pentecostal churches will have you accept and pray to the holy spirit.

I am making an effort to bring you to the Gospel (teachings) of Jesus Christ. What church you choose is up to you. I will not say which Christian church is right or wrong, or better or worse. I will say that I am an American practical protestant Christian (I am a protestant Christian, and I live a practical life), not because I think that is the best way, but for transparency, a gesture of self-disclosure, so that you know where I am coming from, that is what is currently comfortable for myself.

What if one Christian Church is right about its practices, and the other Christian Churches are wrong? There have been wars fought about this between Christians. Politics and corruption have existed in Christian Churches. But, the message of Jesus Christ as the son of God, and the Holy Bible, is real and the same for churches.

Here are some comments regarding conflict from chapter 12 of the book, Interpersonal Persuasion:

"There is a fine line between conflict and persuasion. Resistance to persuasion can lead to open conflict just as open conflict can lead to attempts to persuade. The seeds of conflict are always present in human communication. Persuasion often assumes that there will be winners and losers, elements of compromise and acquiescence, and some degree of conflict…

There are several different kinds of conflict. **Pseudoconflicts** are those where people believe their differing goals cannot be simultaneously achieved. For example, being confronted with a choice between joining friends for pizza and writing a paper is not really a conflict. One could write the paper first and join friends later, leave friends early to write the paper, or exercise countless other options. Pseudoconflicts are sometimes the result of misunderstanding or interpretation. If parents intervened to dictate that you could join your friends when the paper was finished, would that mean when it was outlined, written, or typed? In such instances, solutions to the conflicts seldom require major compromise and provide "win-win" opportunities for the individuals. **Content conflicts** are the most common type of conflict involving disagreement over facts, definitions, goals, or interpretation of information. More interaction often results in mutual understanding and the realization that the differences are not as great as originally perceived. **Ego conflicts** can become the most harmful. Such conflicts are based upon the personalities of the participants. In a sense, each side gets pleasure out of disagreeing with the other side. Participants view themselves as equals in power, knowledge and expertise. The participants feel compelled to advocate and defend specific views or arguments. More interaction alone will have little impact upon solving ego conflicts. **Value conflicts** are the most difficult to solve and, depending upon the values in conflict, can be the most intense or violent.

It would be a mistake to view all conflict as bad. Conflict can establish social international boundaries, reduce tensions, clarify roles, objectives, or differences, and can provide the basis for negotiation and continued interaction."

I don't think that Christianity works that way, where there is a right and a wrong way. The result of the wars is that there are now more choices and places to worship Jesus. I think that the different Christian Churches are like the colors of a rainbow. They are all related, but different. Jesus said, "If they are not against us, they are with us."

What is heaven like? I don't know what heaven is like. It might not be possible for human beings to understand, or comprehend the magnitude of heaven. Jesus talks about heaven when someone asks him what happens if a woman is married and her husband dies, and she marries again. When they die, who will they be with in heaven? Jesus says that things are different in heaven, and in heaven we will be like the angels. Basically, it won't matter who you were married to on Earth.

Paul says that you are born with nothing, and you take nothing with you when you die. Jesus says that heaven is different than Earth, and you won't be the same person. I think the lesson is that the true treasure on Earth is the love you can share with other people on Earth, and the personal relationships you develop on Earth. Most importantly, to prepare yourself for heaven, you should get to know Jesus Christ.

Haiku Holiday

BUKOWSKI'S BUBBLES

"You can do without a woman, but you can't do without a typewriter."
-Charles Bukowski

#59: POETRY: BUKOWSKI'S BUBBLES

(1)
A can's before me.
It has snowy mountain tops.
It's marketing lies.

(2)
25 Ounces
Busch Light comes from Missouri.
No mountains in MO.

(3)
But, It's still good beer.
A perfect beer for watching…
Charles Bukowski read.

(4)
He's the beer poet.
I've got an underground vid.
He reads poetry.

(5)
1970…
He reads in a crowded room,
While drinking a beer.

(6)
So, I drink a beer,
And, I listen to him talk,
About "cocks," and "dykes."

(7)
He talks about life...
Living in Los Angeles,
A drinking poet.

(8)
He reveals his truth;
Hookers and flea bag hotel.
He pontificates.

(9)
He reveals his truth;
Speaking of past, and present;
Betting on horses.

(10)
He talks about sex.
He mixes the romantic,
In concrete cocktail.

(11)
There's an extra ounce,
In this blue white Busch Light can...
Colors of police.

(12)
It's a perfect can,
For a PBJ Cocktail;
Liquid bread sandwich.

(13)
Add 2 tablespoons,
Filled with grape jelly, and stir.
Then... peanut butter.

(14)
That's 2 tablespoons,
Of both, for PBJ beer.
Or, just use jelly.

Haiku Holiday

(15)
He talks about death.
He talks about dying too.
Women... eat that up.

(16)
Death is everywhere.
It is always waiting near.
I pray every day.

(17)
Some people get up.
They walk out of his reading.
Too much death and sex.

(18)
One thing I like, though,
About Charles Bukowski's style,
We both like... cigars.

"The whole world is like this...
Nobody knows what they're supposed to know.
Poets can't write poetry.
Mechanics can't fix your car.
Fighters can't fight.
Lovers can't love.
Preachers can't preach.
It's even like that... with armies..."
-Charles Bukowski

JESUS JOINS THE MAFIA

"Then he said to the disciples, "It is impossible that no offenses [sins] should come [happen, occur], but woe to him [shame on him] through whom they do come! It would be better for him if a millstone were hung around his neck, and he were thrown into the sea, then that he should offend one of these little ones."

What? Did Jesus really say that? That's just like in the movies. "It would be better for him if a millstone were hung around his neck, and he were thrown into the sea, then that he should offend [harm] one of these little ones [children]."

Apparently this practice came from somewhere. Apparently they actually used to do that to people 2000 years ago. Of course... they also used to hang people on crosses to die in public humiliation and pain. I think that I would rather drown than be hung on a cross.

Stop! I do not want to be drown... OR hang on a cross. But... if I had to choose, I would rather drown than hang on a cross. Jesus chose to die for our sins. He was hung on a cross. They hammered nails through his hands and feet and attached him to two posts, and then made him hang from the nails while in the air, until he died six hours later, because he could not breathe any more.

Would you die to save a stranger's life? Most people probably would not. But Jesus did. Jesus died to make a one time sacrifice before God, to pay for or "atone" for, or to make up for, the sins and offenses of man against God.

That is what sin is, an offense that separates us from God... who is perfect. When we sin, we are separated from God. We become imperfect. When we accept the sacrifice of Jesus Christ, by accepting Jesus Christ as our Lord and Savior... and ask Jesus to forgive us, our sins are forgiven before God and we are renewed again and become closer to God... who is perfect.

STOP! Jesus did NOT say to hang a millstone around someone's neck, throw them overboard, and watch them drown as punishment. Jesus did NOT say to do this.

Jesus said, "It is impossible that no offenses [no sins] should come, but woe to him [shame on him] through who they do come."

Jesus said this BEFORE he made his sacrifice on the cross. Jesus was telling us that if we are sinners before God, it will be like drowning with a millstone around your neck when it comes time to face God.

Oh yeah, so THEN, Jesus goes on to tell us what do do… Instead of throwing our enemies overboard.

"Take heed to yourselves. If your brother sins against you, rebuke him; and if he repents, [says he's sorry] forgive him. And if he sins against you seven times in a day, and seven times in a day returns to you saying, "I repent," you shall forgive him.

Then, later, someone asked Jesus, So, I should forgive my brother seven times? And Jesus said no, forgive your brother seven times seven (or something like that). The point is… you should forgive people. Forgive and forget!

WHY SHOULD I BE A CHRISTIAN?

I am going to get to the point. Whatever Christian Church you attend, there are a lot of benefits to being a Christian. The first step, however, is that you have to have faith, or sincerely try to believe to get the "rewards" or benefits.

This is a quick list of a dozen benefits and reasons to be a Christian. There are hundreds of reasons, and I could much more details and examples. But this is a quick and cheap "cheat sheet" of reasons that I could think of.

1). Friends:
By joining a Christian Church, you can make friends and meet people. This can be good for business relationships and networking connections, and for your social life. There are a lot of people that meet their husband or wife in Church. You might pass out your business cards, or get invited to a party.

2). Personality:
By joining a Christian Church, you gain a philosophy that promotes love and acceptance and forgiveness. This can make it easier for you to forgive people, and be nice to people because you have the excuse that you are serving God. When you forgive people and are nice to people and help people, often times, they will forgive you, and be nice to you, and help you too. When you help people, and you serve God, you get a good feeling, improved self esteem, and you feel good about yourself. Christianity can give you a new start, and a new way of life.

3). Purpose:
Christianity is a religion and a philosophy. It offers a moral code. It offers forgiveness of sins, and a belief that when you die, you will live forever with God in the afterlife. Christianity gives you a purpose. It gives you a reason to live. Since you are a Christian, you know that you will be rewarded for serving God in heaven.

4). Identity:
If you are a Christian, it is like you are part of a club. There have been millions of Christians before you, and now you are a part of their club. By becoming a Christian, you can gain the moral advice and guidelines to help you make decisions and find "who you are."

5). Peace:
God offered his son (John 3:16) as a messenger and sacrifice to pay for your sins so you could go to heaven. When you accept Jesus Christ as your Lord and Savior, and believe in him as the Son of God, you will be forgiven of all of your sins when you go to heaven. This is the promise Jesus made several times in the Bible. Whatever happens to you in this life will not be important in heaven. If you get in a car accident and you die, it is like having insurance with God.

6) Advice/Wisdom:
Christianity offers many examples of how to live. Some of this is explained as rules, such as the Ten Commandments. Some examples are told in stories called parables. Some examples are given by the actions of Jesus Christ himself. Jesus offers advice on moral guidelines to live a good life, but also on how to avoid problems and embarrassment, and how to pray to God, and how to stay out of jail, and how to avoid getting killed.

7) Miracles:
Christianity offers access to miracles through the angels and the Holy Spirit. When you accept Jesus Christ as your Lord and Savior, you get the gift of the Holy Spirit, that can provide insight, inspiration, advice, miracles, dreams, and more. Maybe you're really tired, and you need some energy? Maybe you can't get to sleep?

8) Healing:
Doctors have made scientific reports on the healing power of prayer. Some call it a "placebo affect" saying that people trick themselves into feeling better. Still, if prayer works to help heal people, then it doesn't matter how it works. Jesus said that the stronger your faith is, the stronger the miracles and healing you will receive. Jesus healed people many times in the Bible. Jesus gave authority to his disciples to heal people. If you believe in God, and Jesus, and pray for healing, you will be surprised at what you experience.

9) God's Friendship:
Jesus said in the Bible to his disciples, that I have treated you like friends, and not as servants. Jesus offers a personal friendship. You can tell him all of your problems and worries in your prayers. There is a famous hymn (song) called, "What a friend we have in Jesus."

The lyrics to the song explain this:

"What a friend we have in Jesus,
What a friend we have indeed,
What a privilege to carry,
All of our sins to God in need.
Oh what peace we often forfeit.

Oh what needless pain we bear.
All because we do not carry,
everything to God in prayer."

10) Mystical Guidance:
I discussed how Christianity gives access to the Holy Spirit. If you have a problem, you can pray to Jesus and ask for help with the problem. You may get insight from the Holy Spirit. It may come in a dream, or the answer might just pop in your head. Even if you do not get the answer from the Holy Spirit, the act of praying will make you think about what the problem is, and help you find the answer.

11) Leadership:
Both the Old Testament, and the New Testament offer countless examples of leadership. There are stories and examples that can provide motivation, encouragement, and leadership examples. You can use the Bible to give examples to other people when you are required to be a leader. You can quote the Bible to give credibility and strength to what you are telling people.
"This is not just what I think, this is what the Bible says, and this is what other people did before."

12) Courage:
There are countless tales of stressful situations, and times of struggle in the Old Testament, and the New Testament. These can provide examples to give you motivation, encouragement, and courage. You can pray for guidance. And you can pray for God to give you strength (both mental and physical) to face and overcome challenges.

A SIMPLE PRAYER

Jesus gives us the Lord's Prayer, which can be found at Matthew 6:9. But, it is a little long (about 12, or 13 lines). Here is a simple prayer that I do, or you can do both. This prayer is easy to remember because it has only five lines like the five fingers of your hand. And, you can add to it later if you like. Sometimes I will say this prayer before I go to bed at night. Sometimes, I will even repeat it several times.

1. Holy Jesus have mercy.
2. I'm sorry for my sins.
3. Forgive me for my sins.
4. Thank you for my blessings.
5. Praise God, Amen.

Then, you can add things, such as asking for help on line four. I say, "bless me with happy dreams," or "protect me from evil." Or, you can think of the things you are grateful for, such as "Thank you for my health, family, friends, food and shelter, education, and experiences." Try it and see how you feel and sleep. It gives me comfort and peace.

HUMILITY

One of the hardest things to do, is to admit when we're wrong, and ask for forgiveness.
I sent an email to my professor, and I apologized for my comments, for losing my temper, and for the rotten things I said. I explained that I had been under a lot of pressure, and I listed the reasons.

I told her that I hate to tell people, but I'm on probation, and I'm ashamed of it. And I begged her and I begged her to forgive me and let me have an extension to submit the work.
I carefully explained in a short essay, how much I had learned in the class. And, I explained how much hard work I had put in. And, I explained how important the class was to me. And, I explained how grateful I was to be able to be a student. I included quotes from the Bible, and I said I would pray for forgiveness, and I asked her to please have mercy.

I explained that we all make mistakes, and that we can learn from our mistakes, and I would learn from the mistake of missing this assignment and losing my temper. I explained that I am taking anger management counseling. And I asked again, to please, please, let me make it right.

And then, I prayed for real.

DAY EIGHT: THURSDAY

LAUGHING LANGOSTINO

Haiku Holiday

SURPRISE! This Haiku Holiday is LONGER than a week! It was my all time favorite rock and roll band, The Beatles, that said...

"Eight days a week,
I looooooove you!
Eight days a week,
Is not enough to show I care."
-The Beatles (Eight Days a Week)

#60: DESIRE: BUY-SEXUAL BEER

(1)
It's in a green can.
Rock and roll with Rolling Rock.
Latrobe Brewing Co.

(2)
The can has a horse.
It's a green, white and blue can.
It's extra pale ale.

(3)
It's a classic look.
It's from 1939.
It's premium beer.

(4)
They use glass lined tanks.
They use mountain spring water.
25 ounces.

(5)
A horse is a horse.
No one can talk to a horse,
Except Rolling Rock.

(6)
My kingdom for it.
The horse is a mystery.
Number 33?

(7)
Is it a race horse?
Or, is it pony express?
Is it a night mare?

(8)
Is it a mare then?
Or, is it a bold stallion?
Or, is it a knight?

(9)
The beer tastes supreme.
It has a citrus flavor;
An orange, or lime?

(10)
Buy-sexual beer,
Is a name for any beer,
With clams and oysters.

(11)
I'm a hetero.
I might pay for sex some day…
While in New Orleans?

(12)
I knew some pilots,
That said we all pay for it…
Dinner and movie?

(13)
Speaking of movies,
There's the classic, "Spartacus",
With Tony Curtis.

(14)
He's a roman slave,
And they ask him a question…
Do you prefer clams?

(15)
Or, do oysters please?
A co-worker once told me,
It's a sex question.

(16)
But, there's a problem.
I'm not sure, which is which?
The clam's vagina?

(17)
The oyster's anus?
Or, is it the other way?
I… would have to ask.

(18)
That's a BIG mistake!
I prefer oysters, thank you.
NO, CLAMS! I MEAN CLAMS!

(19)
Either way, they're good.
Oysters AND clams, are BOTH good.
They're awesome with beer.

(20)
It is said, oysters…
Are an aphrodisiac.
But clams taste great too!

(21)
They're great, for a date!
Smoked oysters come in a can.
They're great with crackers.

(22)
Clams come in a box,
Frozen with garlic butter.
I would serve them both.

(23)
Top with parmesan,
Served with a cold glass of beer.
It's not expensive.

(24)
Use a tiny fork.
Save the garlic butter sauce.
Put it in the beer.

(25)
Most importantly…
It's better safe, than sorry.
DON'T FORGET CONDOMS!

HENRY MILLER

"Listen, I don't mind what you say about me, but don't make me out to be a cunt-chaser- it's too simple. Some day I'll write a book about myself, and my thoughts. I don't mean just a piece of introspective analysis… I mean that I'll lay myself down on the operating table and I'll expose my whole guts… every goddamned thing. Has anybody ever done that before? What the hell are you smiling at? Does it sound naif?"

I'm smiling because whenever we touch on the subject of
this book which he is going to write someday things assume
an incongruous aspect… The book must be absolutely
original, absolutely perfect. That is why, among other
things, it is impossible for him to get started on it."

-Henry Miller, Tropic of Cancer, p. 132

Haiku Holiday

#61: MIND: I SAID WHAT?

(1)
Henry Miller's great.
He's also… kind of insane.
He exposed… his guts.

(2)
Tropic of Cancer,
That's his most famous project.
He used… the "C" word.

(3)
He wrote down his thoughts.
And, he often said "GD"
Which do you think's worse?

(4)
Most women, get pissed!
If they hear a man say it…
The enflamed "C" word.

(5)
But, many fear… God!
They do not want to see hell!
GD's an insult!

(6)
Miller says it all.
It's cognitive dissonance…
Juxtaposition.

(7)
Vulgar romantic,
Veritas, search for the truth…
High brow, AND Low brow.

(8)
It's a "Uni-brow!"
It's Vulgarity and truth...
Poetry... romance?

(9)
It says all there is,
And, asks a lot of questions.
But... it says too much.

(10)
The "C" word... is "cunt"!
If you're a man... don't say it!
"GD" is Goddamn.

(11)
Tropic of Cancer,
Is like "Catcher" on steroids.
Miller... is crazy!

DENOUEMENT

Dreams are weird. I have recently had a few weird memorable dreams this year. In one dream I was in a car crash. I was hit by another car, and then I woke up. That was very real and weird. In another dream, I was dreaming, and I knew I was dreaming. Then I woke up, but I was still dreaming. And then I woke up for real. So, that has got to be very rare. To be in a dream, and then wake up from the dream... and still be in a dream. Freaky! That has only happened one time.

Recently, I was cooking a barbecue pork shoulder in an electric roast pot. I had never tried this recipe. The barbecue pork is simmered in beer with vegetables and garlic, salt, and pepper for like, eight hours overnight. And, I wanted to check it every two hours to add beer.
So, I set my alarm to go off every two hours during the night. What I discovered, is that I awoke during my rem (rapid eye movement) sleep cycle. This is the deepest stage of sleep, and where one has dreams. So,

by waking every two hours, I was able to remember and experience better dreams. It is something to try.

Now, I do this often on the weekends, or if I do not have a busy day the next day. Recently, I had a dream where I saw Sasquatch! Sasquatch is also known as… Bigfoot! I had a dream where I was on a farm in Iowa, and I was with some people, and I saw Bigfoot walking in an open field. He was GIGANTIC! It was not the Bigfoot that I would have imagined. He was like 20 feet tall! But, I did not see myself in the dream. So, maybe Bigfoot is real, and I was experiencing the view as a mouse, or rabbit, or something. Except, that I was very excited and overjoyed to see Bigfoot, and I shared my excitement and enthusiasm with some other people there. I did not actually see the other people though. Maybe I was being visited by a rabbit ghost from prehistoric times, or the future? Nothing else happened. It was just a brief moment. But, it was very exciting.

I think there is a lesson from this dream. I think that Education, and reading, and seeking knowledge and wisdom are important. But, I think that it is also important to keep your dreams alive and to enjoy your life. Reading the Western Classics, and even the Holy Bible, can be overwhelming and provide access to eternal thoughts. If you read too much, and think too much, you can start to feel your mortality and it can make you feel small. So, I think that it's important to take time to enjoy your life and keep your dreams alive, even if it means being silly or foolish occasionally. The mysteries and wonders of the world can give us inspiration.

What I have learned about myself? What I have come to learn during this week of intensive Haiku writing then, is that through my faith in Jesus Christ, I have received the message that God loves me.

God is BIG. God is REAL. Some think that God has preplanned everything in predestination. Some think that God is an impersonal watchmaker that created the seasons and the days, and leaves it be as a free for all. Some think that God has preselected the "elect" chosen and there is nothing you can do to earn your way to heaven. Some feel that there is Heaven and Hell, and if you are good you go to Heaven, and if you don't follow the rules you go to Hell.

Jason Flick

I believe that God sent Jesus Christ to give us all a free will free choice and a free gift second chance to erase our mistakes through the sacrifice of Jesus Christ on the Cross if we accept him as the Son of God and our Lord. Jesus Christ is the Lamb of God, sacrificed to take away the sins of the world.

God loves us, and wants us to enjoy and experience life as much as we can. That is why he sent his Son, Jesus Christ to provide the message of love, forgiveness, and to give forgiveness of our sins and mistakes so we can be with God in the afterlife. Because… the mysteries and wonders of this life, give us inspiration.

EXIT STAGE LEFT

Overture

"Life imitates art, as art imitates life"
If all the world's a stage, then we live in a cage.
As animals in a zoo, we often engage…
In conflict, thus in ensuing rage
We Kill… Love… Die…
Or age.

Act I (We Kill)

Soft is the flesh, hard ist the steel-
Cold is the instrument, hot is the feel-
Of red warm blood ethereal yet real-
For food, for fun, in fear, or to steal,
Individually… or in numbers, we'll still deal,
In the art of the profane… and call it gentile.

Act II (We Love)

Diamonds, sapphires... gems of the poor.
Stinging, merciless... flaming tongue of the whore.
Victory and defeat, who keeps the score-
Is, doomed to enact an eternal encore-
Piteous and merciful... not just folklore-
For those that know the Truth, salvation is in store.

Act III (We Die)

Metaphysical, mysterious, unknown for sure-
Desired by many... a medical cure-
Feared most by... the purveyors of unpure-
Awaiting their sentence... before the juror.
Those to which this fate did not occur?
The simple, the clean, the benevolent, the demure.

Act IV (We Age)

Graceful, bitter, ambitious, or dry-
The sultry shadows of youth go by-
Uninhibited they frolic and dance and reach for the sky
Still far too many choose to deny-
These joys of life, instead they lie,
Rotting and stagnant... waiting to die.

Denouement

The curtain reveals all is not what it may seem.
Callous and empirical... absolute and extreme,
Is our refusal... to accept... the universal theme.
The players- good and evil, the divine existence supreme.
Thus awakens man's mental slumber from before the Nicene
The last apple... "to sleep, perchance to dream..."

Jason Flick

THINKING THOUGHTS

As I sit comfortably in a department store sofa chair, and I listen placidly to the soft lingering echoes of the department store pianist strumming her magic on the department store baby grand piano, I find myself contemplating my existence on the planet. I think back to living in New York. And, I think back to living in Los Angeles. Although I am grateful for having lived in these enchanting locations, I can say without modesty that I succeeded in failing miserably at finding my "niche."

So, now as I contemplate my existence, and my future, I ask myself, Was it my own actions that caused this failure? Or, was it predestined? Could I have changed my behaviors to accommodate the local culture? Was I naively being judgmental, by separating myself and not fitting in? Or, was this a long journey to discovering how and when to be myself… and the benefits and timing of, NOT being myself.

Haiku Holiday

THE PRICKLY ROAD

What has led me to this destiny?
This is never what I thought I would be.
Alone and walking on a desert highway,
Striving for a golden city that is someday,
I keep walking, and walking, and walking.
I keep talking, and talking, and talking,
To myself, to remind me that I'm alive.
The lights of Las Vegas in the distance,
Seem to thrive.

Will it be all that was promised?
Will it be all that I imagined?
Will I have my hopes and dreams fulfilled-
When I arrive?

Or, is it just another El Dorado;
A utopian city of gold…
That doesn't exist?
Why do I keep going forward alone?
Why do I try to resist,
The calls of the harpies alongside the road;
That sing so sweetly with temptations of delight.
They beg me to stop, stay, rest, and unload;
"To sleep, perchance to dream," and drift into the night.

I hear one particular voice;
A sweet feminine call.
She reminds me softly,
"This was your choice."

Jason Flick

THE ROPE

This is a separate poem, about despair and hope. Actually that rhymes with rope, so that should have been a line in the poem, but this is not the poem. Even though I'm not currently Roman Catholic, one could make a metaphor between "Rope", and "Pope". This poem is about, "amazing grace." Grace means God's forgiveness. Also, this poem is not a haiku. But, I promise to end this book with a "happy" haiku.

THE ROPE

I woke up and felt a drop of sweat on my face.
I was standing on a cliff over a sea of disgrace.
There was a cloud of vultures circling around me.
They were shouting directions,
About what to do and who to be.

There was nothing I could do.
There was nothing I could say.
There was nothing that would make them go away.
So, I got down on my knees and I started to pray.
And, this is what I heard the Lord say…

From high up above, there came a rope.
I heard a voice say, "Come on, there's no time to mope.
It's time to grab on and learn to cope.
Just pull yourself up…
and don't give up hope."

The rope was long.
The rope was high.
Sometimes it seemed to disappear into the sky.
I prayed to the Lord, I asked him why?
Why is life so hard? Why do I feel like I want to die?

He said, "It's okay to feel bad.
It's okay to cry.
But, it's not okay to just sit and lie.
Because you'll never know the answers unless you try.
There WILL come a day, when you get to fly!"

GOOD NEWS

GOOD NEWS! I passed! I passed my drug test! I got a call from my probation officer.
"We did receive communication from the court, that your case has been terminated, your term has ended. So, we are closing your case here. You will get your discharge in the mail. We don't need any more communication back and forth. So, I hope you have a good life."

Yeah, it's done. And, I received an email from my professor regarding my apology and request for an incomplete in the course. She accepted my apology, and is going to allow me an extension to submit my last assignment.

And, I SOLD MY CAR! I got a visit from the perfect buyer. A young lady, she just crashed her car, and needed a new one as soon as possible. It's a good car for her... with airbags.
It's a great car, and she can afford it. She paid cash!

And, since I got released from probation, I called an ex-girlfriend... and she and her boyfriend just broke up! She's on the rebound! I told her, I just sold my car, and I want to celebrate. We're going to go out. I am sooo going to get laid... I hope. It'll be fun, anyway. There's a hot new modern bowling alley that just opened up, and we're going to go bowling. Lots of room for sex jokes when bowling. There are big shiny balls... big bulbous round pins... Shoes! There are shoes! Now, I have to find a job.

The bad news, is that... I forgot my motherfucking son of a bitch password! My next password will be a dirty word... "Fuck Face," or "Stupid Password." I should remember that.

Jason Flick

I BELIEVE IN ME

Oops, I guess I did use that rhyme with hope and rope in that last poem. This is a separate poem. It says, I believe in me. This does not mean that you should not believe in Jesus. It just means that God loves you, and wants you to love yourself.

I BELIEVE IN ME

Sometimes you will fall.
Sometimes you will stand.
Sometimes for help, you will call.
Sometimes you will lend a hand.

But if there is one thing I have learned;
One thing I think you will agree,
No matter how people are concerned,
You must say, "I believe in me!"

Sometimes you will fail.
Sometimes you will be wrong.
Those are the times to be strong,
And, try to sing a new song.

#62: WILL: THANK YOU JESUS

(1)
Holy Jesus Christ,
Please forgive me for my sins.
Glory be to God!

POST SCRIPT

DRUNK PUPPY

#63: SOUL: THE BOTTLE OF CHRIST

(1)
99 bottles
99 bottles of beer
That sit on the wall.

(2)
When you take one down
And then you pass it around
There's 98 left.

(3)
But when Christ's in town,
Take one and pass it around.
There's still 99!

(4)
And it's the BEST BEER!
That you could ever think of.
The bottle of Christ.

#64: GOD: Unfinished

I have left the God haiku unfinished, because you need to find your own path to faith in God. I believe in a personal relationship with Jesus Christ as the Son of God. There are many religions in this World. There are many versions of Christianity. Some people believe that these different religions are different paths to God. Jesus says that He is the one true path to God. I choose him as my Lord and Savior, or perhaps, he has chosen me. But, I think that we all have the free will to make our own choices. And, I think that we should all try to appreciate and respect each other, however we choose to seek God. God bless you, and peace be with you.

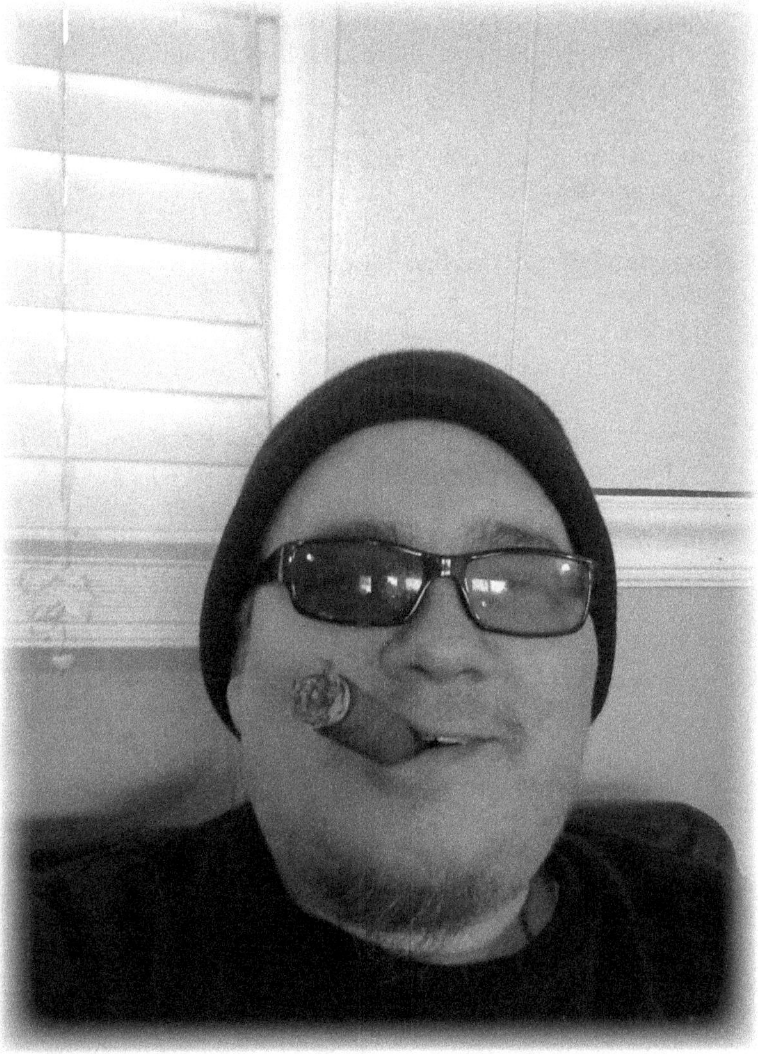

WORKS CITED

Adler, M., Van Doren, C. *How to Read a Book: The Classic Guide to Intelligent Reading.* Touchstone Book Published by Simon & Schuster, New York, 1972.

Adler, M. *Six Great Ideas.* Macmillan Publishing Co., Inc. New York, 1981.

Biggs, D. *Cocktails.* Crescent Books. New York. 1995

Fadiman, C. *The Lifetime Reading Plan.* Avon Book Division. The Hearst Corporation. New York, N.Y.

Jones, J., Wilson, W. *An Incomplete Education, Third Edition.* Ballantine Books, New York, 2006

Luck, S. The Complete Guide to Cigars. Parragon Books Ltd., New York, 2008

McGeveran, W., Lazzara, E., Wiesenfeld, L., Seabrooke, K., Spadafora, V., Meyerhofer, M., Et. Al. *The World Almanac and Book of Facts 2005.* World Almanac Books. New York, 2005

Riccio, B. *Walter Lippmann-Odyessy of a Liberal.* Transaction Publishing, New Brunswick, New Jersey, 1994

Soukhanov, A., Jost, D., Ellis, K., Severynse, M., Berube, M., Latimer, J., Pickett, J., Pritchard, D., Weeks, D., Patwell, J., Et. Al. *The American Heritage Dictionary of The English Language, Third Edition.* Houghton Mifflin Company, Boston, 1992

Stearns, P., Schwartz, D., Beyer, B., Salter, C., *World History Traditions and New Directions.* Addison-Wesley Publishing Company, Inc., New York, 1989

Ford, G., Ford, C., Rollins, A., Millar, R., Stevers, M., Jones, S. Et Al. *Compton's Pictured Encyclopedia*. F.E. Compton & Company, Chicago, 1957

Gideons International, *The Holy Bible (King James Version)*. National Publishing Company, Nashville, 1978

Wong, S., Spector, S. *The Complete Idiot's Guide to Gambling Like a Pro, Third Edition*. Pearson Education Inc., Indianapolis, 2003

Zakaras, A., Paik, K., White, E., Davidson, T., Halpern, G., Mahajan, Manjari., Sheppard, B., *Let's Go Europe 1999*. St. Martin's Press, New York, 1999

Printed in the USA
CPSIA information can be obtained
at www.ICGtesting.com
LVHW091057311223
767829LV00007B/110